THE SEVERED HEAD

Camp Mudjokivi

KOINONIA

Owl Woods

Path to Telanoo

Wildflower Meadow

Tree House Village

Outer Cabins

Frog Lagoon

The Shelter

Rocky Creek

Old Pilgrim Church

Silver Lake

Ropes Course

Old Road

Lake Gazebo

Paddleboat Dock

The Pool

Lodge

Nature Center

Family Cabins

The Morgan Farm

Small Gazebo

Elijah's House

Dining Hall

Maintenance Building

MUDJOKIVI

Staff Apartments

N
W   E
S

Elijah Creek & The Armor of God #1

The Severed Head

Lena Wood

Standard®
PUBLISHING
Cincinnati, Ohio

Published by Standard Publishing, Cincinnati, Ohio
www.standardpub.com

Project editor: Lindsay Black
Content editor: Amy Beveridge
Copy editor: Lynn Lusby Pratt
Cover and interior design: Robert Glover
Cover photography: Robert Glover
Cover oil paintings: Lena Wood
Map illustration: Daniel Armstrong
Scripture taken from the HOLY BIBLE, NEW INTERNATIONAL
VERSION®. NIV®. Copyright © 1973, 1978, 1984 by International
Bible Society. Used by permission of Zondervan. All rights reserved.

Library of Congress Cataloging-in-Publication Data

Wood, Lena, 1950-
    The severed head / Lena Wood.
        p. cm. — (Elijah Creek & the Armor of God ; bk. 1)
    Summary: When Elijah and his friends find a treasure in an abandoned
church, they discover that God has plans for them that they never expected.
    ISBN 0-7847-1583-1 (pbk.)
    [1. Christian life—Fiction. 2. Friendship—Fiction.] I. Title.
PZ7.W84973Se 2005
[Fic]—dc22

                                                                    2004009149

ISBN-13: 978-0-7847-1583-3
ISBN-10: 0-7847-1583-1

15 14 13 12 11 10 09   4 5 6 7

to **Mom** *and* **Dad**
for loving the land and the Word

Deepest appreciation to:
Zach Hudson, Sam Wright, *and*
Robbie McMath, *cover models*
Cason *and* **Danielle Pratt** *and*
Wayne Keith, *camp staff advisers*
Dan Dyke, *biblical language adviser*
Masumi Snyder, *Japanese language and culture consultant*
Arian Brooke *and* **Andrea Summer,**
love and support
&
Yahweh, *the* **Greatest Spirit,** *everything*

Chapter 1

NEVER—not in my wildest dreams—did I ever imagine that an innocent peek into an old church would change my life forever, turning me into the wild vagabond I am now. But it did.

My name is Elijah Creek, and I descended from the Creek Indians—at least I always hoped so. My dad's family came from southern Georgia where the Creek nation lived. We didn't know where mom came from. She was adopted. But since her hair and eyes are dark, I thought she might be Indian too.

Sometimes I wonder what would have happened if I hadn't volunteered as a stagehand for the junior high play. We were doing *The Adventures of Tom Sawyer*. I wanted to be Injun Joe—I had the dark hair and eyes for the role—but I can't act.

My cousin Robbie . . . now he could act. We were nothing alike, and I mean nothing. I lived in a log house in Camp Mudjokivi, a nature camp my dad ran. Robbie lived in what everyone in town called The Castle. It was old and drafty and had a tower with mice—or worse—living in the walls. His parents had plans to make it into a bed-and-breakfast, but I hadn't seen much progress. It looked more like Bates Motel from the movie *Psycho*.

Robbie was ready to turn fourteen but could have passed for eleven. I called him Chunk. He called me Rail. He sings and acts; I draw a little. I've always liked the wild outdoors, while he's an indoor person and likes studying history and stuff. So he's not the coolest cube in the tray. But we got along.

That fall, Robbie had roped some of us into helping with costumes, set building, and the dangerous work of hanging lights, curtains, and backdrops. We'd been through our basements and attics, searching for curtains and costumes and backdrops, but with no luck.

Reece Elliston called me after an hour of searching and said, "No luck here. All our curtains are hanging in windows, and we don't have any pioneer-type dresses."

"We're going to have to branch out," I said. "Robbie had an idea that the old church may have some curtains. Want to check it out?"

"Sure. Can Mei come too?"

When Reece did anything, Mei wasn't far behind. They were opposites too. Mei had dark eyes and short dark hair to Reece's long blond hair and blue eyes. Mei was shy while Reece spoke her mind. I think they struck up a friendship because they were a little different from everyone else: Mei's from Japan, and was still working on her English. Reece had this bone condition, and sometimes had to use a cane.

By the time all of us—Robbie and me, Reece and Mei— were done with dinners and homework and had met up on my porch, it was nearly dark. The days were getting shorter already.

The only reason I hadn't explored the church was because

it was condemned and Dad said no. But I hadn't asked about it for a long time.

Old Pilgrim Church and the graveyard behind it sat on a grassy hill surrounded by an overgrown meadow and woods, west of Camp Mudjokivi where I lived. The camp hooked up with the Morgan farm to the east. To the north was a big scary hunk of land I named Telanoo, which sounds Indian, and is short for The Land No One Owns. Owl Woods, the camp's nature preserve, bled over into Telanoo.

Mom was upstairs with the twins, so I asked my dad if we could investigate the old church, and first he said no, it could be dangerous. Then right in the middle of our conversation the phone rang and while he was talking I mouthed the words, "I'll be careful," as I backed out of the house. So he nodded and waved me off. I have lots of duties around camp, and Dad pretty much lets me have the run of the place because he knows I'm responsible.

The old church was locked. But one of the basement windows was broken so it wasn't really like breaking in, though Reece said it was.

I kicked out the rest of the glass and checked for sharp edges where I'd be crawling through. Before going in I turned to Reece. "You don't think God will strike me with lightning, do you?" I liked kidding Reece about her religion.

She grinned. But then she threw in, "You'll probably be okay. Just don't slash an artery on that broken glass."

Reece—for all her sweetness—has an acid streak. And just when you least expect it, she'll get a dig in. She seems fragile because of her looks—she's small and sort of pale—but she's not.

I dropped into the church basement. There was barely enough twilight coming in to see my way up the stairs. I reached out the broken window for Robbie's flashlight. He was chickening out already. I could see it on his face.

"Forget it," I said and sent him and the girls around to the front door. I'd been training myself to see better at night, but on my way through the basement and up the stairs I heard skittering noises from one of the dark corners: big sounds, not so different from the ones Robbie and I hear in the walls at The Castle. I couldn't see what it was. Pretty creepy.

By the time they got to the front door, I'd unbolted it from the inside. We lost most of the natural light in that few minutes, but we went prowling anyway. The girls stayed close to Robbie because he had the flashlight. Reece can't afford to fall and break anything, so I warned them that the floor slanted down to the front stage. There was hardly anything inside except for a few rows of old fold-down seats. The place was musty smelling and a weird kind of cold, even though outside was warm and mellow.

"Usually there would be a velvet curtain in front of the baptistery," whispered Reece, as we crept toward the stage, "and some short curtains in front of the choir loft. The railing is still there, but someone must have taken the curtains when the church closed. Let's check downstairs. Some old churches use curtains as classroom dividers."

We made our way to the stairs. "Don't be afraid if you see a mouse, or a rat," I cautioned. "I heard noises down there."

Reece turned to Mei and whispered, "Mice, maybe. *Daijoubu.*"

"It is all right," Mei said. She and Reece often swapped words. Reece would say it in Japanese, then Mei would say it in English, or vice versa, to learn each other's language.

It's amazing how quick it gets dark, once the sun drops into the woods.

I helped Reece down to the basement where there was nothing more than three squares of gray light coming through the windows—one minus all its glass—and Robbie's flashlight.

"Hold it steady," I told him. "You're going to rattle all the life out of it."

Something scratched at the floor behind us. Reece and Mei sucked in air.

Robbie whispered, "Let's go."

"Why are you whispering, silly?" I asked loudly, kicking at a piece of trash on the floor. "Let's show those rats we're here." I was talking and kicking my way into being the brave one. My mind knew there was nothing to be afraid of, but my heart was thumping. "This was your idea anyway, Robbie. We'll have one quick look around and be done."

In a minute we were stuck together like one person with eight shuffling feet and four heads. Four pairs of eyes bugged out, trying to pick details out of the dark. We followed Robbie's shaky flashlight beam around the room: just cement block walls oozing ground water and three or four doors.

"Classrooms," Reece whispered, nodding toward the doors.

I had just said that whispering was dumb. Obviously, she hadn't taken my lead.

"Classrooms, yeah, I know," I said, though as far as churches went, I really didn't know the layout.

There was pretty much nothing downstairs, except for a rusty furnace at the far end, and what looked like a door behind it made of painted planks. Reece spotted the door too.

"Storage," I guessed.

"Probably," she said.

We all moved as a clump in that direction and watched the door for a minute. Robbie's eyes were like glass marbles. I could tell he was more than ready to leave.

"Let's look in there," I said.

"It is okay?" Mei asked.

"It's okay," I said, and shook the others off. "If there are any curtains, I bet they'll be in there."

The door was swollen shut with dampness and age, but a few good yanks and we were suddenly looking into a low, pitch-black room with a dirt floor.

"It's a crawl space," I said.

Robbie moved the beam slowly around the wall. There were no shelves or boxes, only large hooks embedded in the stone walls.

"Hooks," Robbie breathed.

I knew what he was thinking: torture chamber. But they were just for hanging stuff on.

On the left wall was a doorway, or rather a place broken open in the damp stones, big enough for someone to walk through. Robbie's flashlight beam danced on that black hole. None of us wanted to go any farther. What was in there? I just had to know.

"Come on." My voice had dropped into a whisper despite my best effort. We were in a clump again, moving toward the hole . . . through the hole . . . into a small, damp room. Robbie's light dipped to the dirt floor. The girls gasped. My heart—which was already thumping at fifty miles a minute— jumped into my throat and lodged there. Along the far wall there was a mound of dirt, human size: rounded at the top, squarish at the bottom.

I could barely even breathe the words: "A grave."

We were all frozen in place for a moment. What happened next would shove my heart back down into my chest and throw every muscle into superhuman speed and strength mode. From somewhere behind us came a sound soft as a whisper . . . *scuff* . . . *scuff* . . . *scuff*. . . . Immediately my mind whirled back to the minute before when I was practically yelling, and suddenly I wished I'd kept my big mouth shut. Somebody was out there and unless they were deaf, they knew exactly where we were: in a makeshift mausoleum with only one way out.

Chapter 2

IDEAS flipped through my mind like a deck of cards. I grabbed Robbie's hand and turned off the flashlight, throwing us into pitch dark. We could make a run for it, except for Reece, and I'd have to carry her. I'd noticed Mei going stiff as a board as I flipped off the light. *I might have to carry her too.*

There was one more *scuff,* then the sound stopped.

He knows we're here, I thought to myself. I figured he was about halfway across the basement, between us and the stairs.

My eyes adjusted and fixed on the patch of gray that was the doorway. My ears stayed cued. I hoped with every pounding in my chest that a dark shape wouldn't move into that gray doorway. I had no weapon. The flashlight was still in Robbie's hand, and if I grabbed it again, he'd think I was *him* and die right there, or worse, start screaming like a banshee.

Scuff scuff . . . snt-snt-snt. The sound was getting fainter. He was leaving, tiptoeing up the stairs. I thought, *Maybe he has no right to be here either. Maybe we're no more intruders than him . . . or it . . . or whatever.* I'm not a real believer in ghosts, but in a church basement grave in the murky dark, when your knees turn to jelly, so does your brain. But I was in charge, so it was up to me to take the lead.

All quiet.

None of us moved.

"Stay," I whispered. "Give me the flashlight."

I took it from Robbie's hand, crept out into the basement, turned the flashlight on and swept the room. Nothing. "Let's go!" I whispered back to the others.

There was a scuffle behind me, and in a second Robbie was pressed against my back, Mei behind him. I curled my arm around Reece, half carrying her as we flew across the church basement and up the stairs. We were light as feathers on those old planks. Reece's feet hardly touched the floor.

I turned the flashlight off right before we got outside. The moon was just above the trees, in gibbous stage, making the lake a shimmery sheet before us. The light of the moon above and its reflection on water below washed the landscape of the camp in phosphorous magic. I breathed in relief at the sight of it. Scared as I was, we were really only a few hundred yards from home. I peeked around the corners of the old church. No one was running down to the lake, or through the graveyard to the north. And the open meadow with woods beyond on the side farthest from camp—empty. Whoever he was, he had disappeared like mist.

Reece was breathing hard. I took a few gulps of air myself. Mei sniffled and looked at Reece and kept repeating something in Japanese that sounded like tie-hen. I think Robbie was crying, at least on the inside. We were over the fence and on our way to the lake path when he burst out with a flood of questions.

"Who was that?" he asked. "Do you think he knew we were there? There's somebody buried in there, Elijah!! What are we gonna do? A murder! I can't believe it! A murderer at Camp Mudj?!"

"Shhh! Come on!" I said. "To the lodge!"

I led the way, since I know every square inch of the camp, every gopher hole and every dip in the trail. I kept looking back, wondering how that man or creature or whatever it was could have vanished like that.

There'd been a staff meeting in the lodge earlier, so the fire was still going, but down to embers. The only other lights were the red exit signs above the doors. We got Reece a pillow and sat on the floor. I tossed a log on the fire.

"We've got to go back," I said.

Mei's eyes got wide and she made an owl-type moan. "Noooooo. Terrible!"

"*Taihen!*" Reece cried.

"Not tonight," I corrected, "later. Tomorrow. By light of day."

Reece had caught her breath by now. "We were trespassing and we got caught."

"We didn't get caught!" I said.

"We did!" she snapped.

"Whoever he was, he left when he heard us, so he had no business being there either," I defended.

"Somebody's buried in that room!" said Robbie, his eyes glowing orange from the embers.

Costumes and curtains seemed much less important than looking for a church phantom and doing a little digging in that basement. But here was the problem: a full schedule of events at Camp Mudjokivi. It would be risky to get back into the basement without being seen; a hundred squealing kids from Newpoint and Northwest Elementary schools were scheduled for an overnighter. They'd be swarming the place with leaf books, butterfly nets, and bug boxes. (It's a wonder Camp Mudj hasn't been picked clean by now, with all those bugs getting regularly carted off to their doom.) A church group was coming for a "prayer retreat" at the lodge too. Camp was booked solid.

We stared at the fire. The girls would back out, I figured. But I wasn't going by myself. Robbie might need some arm-twisting. I could see in his eyes that raccoon-stuck-on-the-screen-door look, a "What in the world was I thinking, how did I get myself here?" kind of look. I almost laughed.

"I'll do the digging," I coaxed. "And if I . . . hit . . . anything . . ." I paused. Robbie turned a little green, so I added, "Hey, you know, it could be buried treasure."

"Oh sure," he said sarcastically. "The pirates of Ohio with their gold doubloons and pieces of eight—buried in the shape of a body. Right."

"Other people than pirates bury treasures!" I defended.

"Like who?"

"Rich people who don't trust their relatives. And . . . and eccentric old women with thirty cats and stuff like that.

I'm just saying we don't know what's there until we dig. It just doesn't make sense to bury a body there when there's a cemetery right out the back door."

"Maybe he makes it look like body, so no one touch it," Mei suggested.

"Good thinking," Reece told Mei. "This is dangerous, Elijah."

Mei nodded. "Maybe we should not touch it."

"Well, I'm not digging," Robbie said, crossing his arms.

"And I said you don't have to. You hold the flashlight."

"I may not even watch."

"I don't care."

He slumped a little, like he was giving in. I was ready to do it by myself, if necessary. But I really needed someone to come with me . . . to hold the light.

Chapter 3

※※

IT ate at me, wondering what was in that basement, but I finished out the week of school and waited for the elementary kids and the prayer retreat people to leave. Aunt Grace, Uncle Dorian, and Robbie came over for Sunday brunch. My cousin had mustered his courage by then. While they had coffee and dessert, we got ready to go.

Then it poured rain and the lodge roof started leaking again. Dad had us moving buckets around for the rest of the afternoon.

"Did you find what you needed in the old church?" Dad asked out of the blue as we mopped up the last of the leaks and put chairs out in rows.

Robbie kept his head bent to the task of mopping, but shot me a look.

"Nah," I said casually. "Nothing there. It was a bust."

"I don't know what you're looking for . . ."

"Curtains, backdrops. Big stuff to paint or hang. We have to come up with the play scenery ourselves."

"There's some canvas from that party tent that fell to pieces. It's still in the maintenance building, stored with the lumber."

"Thanks. We'll take a look at it," I said.

"What was in the old church?" he asked curiously.

"Nothing, Dad. Just a few seats. That's all."

"And rats and ghosts," Robbie said with a fake laugh.

"Should be torn down, really. Or burned . . . dangerous old eyesore," Dad said, surveying the ceiling for drips. "The fire department could use it for practice."

Robbie and I eyed each other and brain-waved *uh-oh.*

From the window in my room, I'd kept a nightly stakeout on the church with my binoculars for as long as I could stay awake. The gibbous moon had grown to full and gave good light, except when night clouds turned the whole camp to one big shadow.

On Monday after homework and dinner, Robbie and I set out for the old church. Clouds were low and purple and heavy. Heat from the lake had made a fog. Twilight came early.

I couldn't get him past the fence.

We squatted there behind a hedge of Virginia creeper vines, which separated camp from church property—him with the flashlight and a sock cap over his blond hair, me with a shovel—just staring at Old Pilgrim Church while the purple clouds overhead got lower and darker.

Finally, out of frustration, I leaped the vine-covered wire fence and left him hunkered down by himself. I hoped he'd follow, from loneliness if nothing else.

"C'mon. Let's go. If we get in any kind of trouble, I'll take the—" I broke off when a movement up the hill caught my eye.

Chapter 3

A hunched, sickly silhouette with a cone of light coming out of his belly moved through the fog. It was an old man creeping from the church with a flashlight in one hand, a sack and a long stick in the other. In a minute I could make out that the stick was actually a shovel. Robbie had stood and reared back to make the leap over the fence, so I jabbed a finger in the direction of the old church. He spotted the old man and froze. I shoved him back down behind the fence.

Stashing myself as far into the Virginia creepers as I could, I was still in plain sight if the man—not a hundred yards away—should look my way.

Don't look, I thought. *Don't look, don't look.*

Fog and clouds had turned Camp Mudjokivi from a fun nature camp into one of those old black-and-white horror movies. The old man made his way through the tombstones and stopped. He put the sack down and started digging. This was going to take a while.

"'Lijah!" Robbie whispered through the fence.

"Can you see him?" I asked.

"Sort of."

"Stay put."

"'Kay."

Time passed. My leg went to sleep, so I poked at it to wake it up. I had to be ready to run, just in case. I pictured myself trying to get away, dragging one leg behind me through the fog like in an old mummy movie, and nearly got tickled, in spite of my predicament. I wasn't really too scared. After all, what could one old man do to me?

He was digging a pretty deep hole, though the sack wasn't big enough for a whole body. I started getting the creeps thinking about what might be in that sack, and hoped Robbie wasn't thinking the same thing.

Don't come calling for me, Mom, I said in a prayer to the air. *I'm okay.*

Finally the old man put his shovel down and started messing with the sack. I fought off getting sick when he pulled out a limp arm and dropped it in the hole. Then he pulled out something round—a head!

He held it in his hands, looking at it for a minute as if to tell it good-bye, and then dropped it in the hole too.

He started shoveling again, more hurriedly and with a lot of scraping noises.

"Did you see? . . ." came a little mouse voice through the creeper vines.

"Yeah," I whispered back.

"A head!"

"Yeah . . ."

"And an arm!"

"Shhh!"

"He murdered someone and stuck 'em in the church until—"

"Shhh!" I said again.

Sometimes fog conducts sound. If we could hear every scrape of his shovel, I reckoned he might be able to hear our whispers, even above night sounds from the woods and cars on the road headed toward town. He threw the sack into the grave, shoveled a few more minutes, and wiped his forehead with the back of his hand. He went back through the tombstones just the way he'd come, now dragging the shovel behind him. He stopped once, looked back at the cemetery, and brought his shoulders up, then down, like he was heaving a big sigh.

Then he looked in our direction.

I tried to be invisible by very slowly inching my way even farther under the vines, careful not to snap a twig or crunch a leaf. *Quiet, Robbie,* I kept saying in another air prayer, *don't freak out. He's not looking at us, but above our heads at the lake. That's all. He's done the deed and he's feeling satisfied. Whatever you do, don't throw up!*

Fog glided up from the lake and swallowed the old man just before he went behind the church. I took the opportunity to leap back over the fence . . . and came down on Robbie's back.

For me it was like landing on a tight, sweaty roll of sleeping bags. For him it must have been like getting showered with an armload of baseball bats. My worst fear at that second was that Robbie would yell and give us away. But even as my knees and elbows punched holes in him, Robbie went facedown into the ground with a quiet "Ghhhfmm." It was admirable.

I rolled off him and landed on one knee, puzzled for a second as to where my other knee was.

Somehow my right foot had gotten stuck in the fence. For a really awkward few seconds I was stuck there, my arms thrown out for balance, one knee lodged in the damp ground, one leg stretched out behind me. I bet I looked ridiculous, like a water fountain statue without the fountain.

I yanked my foot free from the wire fence, and down I hurtled, head over heels. There we were, spread-eagled side by side, him facedown, me faceup on the grass. We didn't move. We listened. I turned my eyes up the hill for any hint of a beam of light coming our way.

"You okay?" I asked.

He panted a couple of times. "Yeah. Did you see that? It's a murder! We've got to call the cops!"

"Hold on. Shhh. He's still in the church. He may be able to—"

"Elijaaah!"

My heart thudded to a stop. Mom's voice rang across all hundred acres of the camp and into the next county.

I was on my feet in half a second, flying down the hill to the lake like I had wings, hoping Robbie was behind me. If Mom could catch sight of me, she'd stop calling; if not, I had about five seconds before her voice would ring out again, loud enough to rattle the windows in Old Pilgrim Church. I hoped the old man didn't hear. He was still in the basement probably, putting the shovel away . . . or digging up the rest of—

"Elijaaah!"

Drats!

Heart pounding, legs burning, I zipped along the lake path, then cut back up the hill toward home, wishing there was woods or a building between Old Pilgrim Church and me, or that the fog would swallow me. The main part of the camp was a bowl shape. Sound carried. Every morning we'd hear old Mr. Morgan sneeze, regular as a rooster at dawn, from his back porch through the strip of woods way on the other side of camp. Through that broken basement window, I was betting the old grave digger could hear our feet pounding the pavement of the lake path, and Mom yelling my name, clear as a bell.

I glanced back. The church was little more than a black cutout on a gray background, the tombstones little tabs drifting through the creeping fog. Robbie stumbled up the hill behind me, panting and holding his side.

I dashed the last hundred yards of the driveway. Mom was on the porch. I waved and she waved back, happy to see me but annoyed. "Elijah, I forgot about the PTO meeting. We have to leave in five minutes or we'll be ridiculously late," she said, tossing her long hair, digging keys out of her purse. "Change clothes and bring your homework."

"I already did my homework."

She opened the screen for us. "The first PTO meeting of the school year tends to run long. And the play meeting! You didn't tell me about that."

"I'm just a stagehand."

"But I think you're supposed to be there, and Robbie's in the cast. Grace called wondering where he is. She's on her way there now. Didn't you have a note or something about it? I couldn't get a baby-sitter on such short notice, so if your meeting about the play gets done early, you can watch the girls and do your homework in the back of the commons."

"I already did my—"

"Girls! Time to go!" she called up the steps. "You're muddy, Robbie. Have you boys been wrestling?"

Bounding up to my room, proud of the speed of my long legs, I had changed clothes before Robbie could drag his short self up the stairs.

"You ran off and left me out there!" Robbie wheezed.

"Did not! I had to get to Mom before she gave us away."

"Did he see us?"

"Nah."

He ran a hand over his blond head. "My cap! It's out there!"

"We'll get it later." I shoved a book into my pack and rooted around my desk for a couple of pencils. Mom seemed determined that I still had homework to do. Better to play along.

"What if he saw us?" Robbie asked. "What if he knows that we saw what he did?"

"He doesn't know who we are."

"If he heard your mom call you, then he knows your name."

A chill ran down my spine, but I kept my voice steady. "He'd think I was a camper, one of a hundred."

"We should call the cops," Robbie said, still panting as he scraped mud off his pants leg with his thumbnail.

He was right. I knew that. But I slung my pack over my shoulder and snapped, "We're not leaking a word, not until we've thought this over. Sleep on it, okay. Lock your doors and windows tonight and just sleep on it. Something just doesn't make sense."

We raced down the steps. I made sure the door was locked behind me, though in Magdeline, Ohio, we hardly ever bother. But this time I locked it, because as we'd dashed past the nature center and the lodge, what I saw—and what I wish I hadn't seen—was the grave digger man standing on the stoop of that old wreck of a building, staring pretty much in my direction.

I couldn't let my imagination run away. There was no way of knowing if he saw us. It was pretty dark. He might have been staring down at the lake, like before, very pleased with himself.

We were probably okay, I said to myself. *Yeah, we're okay.*

Chapter 4

ROBBIE ran up to me in the school hallway the next day. "So!?"

"I don't know yet."

"You said you'd sleep on it. Did you find my cap?"

"I didn't sleep much, and no. It's probably still at the fence." I'd spent a good deal of the night watching out the window, grateful I was safe on the second floor, glad that the house stairs creaked when anyone climbed them.

"Hi."

Reece and Mei were waiting at my locker.

"Hi."

I tried to put on my best face, but it was too late. Reece picks up on people's looks—she can almost tell what they're thinking. It's spooky how good she is at it.

"What's wrong?" she asked.

"Wrong?" I asked innocently. "I'm still looking for costumes, if that's what you mean. No luck yet."

Kind of a lie, and the last thing on my mind. But sort of true.

Reece rolled her eyes like I'd insulted her.

Robbie looked at me and I looked back at him. We had to tell them or they'd just keep pecking at us like hens until we did.

"Gather in," I said. We made a huddle in front of my

locker. Robbie and I took turns summing up what happened, except for me telling the part about seeing the old man on the church stoop afterwards looking like he saw us, and about losing sleep over what it all meant. That could wait.

"You have to call the police!" Reece said.

"We don't know it was a murder," I defended.

"People who lose a head and an arm usually die," she said sarcastically.

"It was the shape of a head and arm, but we don't know—"

"Buried in a graveyard?! What do you think it is, a bowling ball and a . . . a . . . arm-shaped thing!?"

"Okay, okay! Keep your voice down."

The last thing we needed was a bunch of other kids with appetites for treasure or detective work listening in, wanting a piece of the action.

Mei politely warned, "The bell will ring."

Reece nodded Mei on to her class and winced as she turned herself down the hall. She had her cane today. I couldn't help wondering if the escape from the church—me dragging her up the steps and across the camp last week—had been too much of a strain. I suddenly felt guilty, remembering how I'd crossed the camp last night in roughly fourteen seconds— like I had wings. She'd never be able to run like that, free as a bird. I couldn't think about it.

I followed her and whispered in her ear. "Hey, don't say anything about this, okay. Let's all decide together. Whatever we do, Reece, you're a part of it, okay?"

She stopped and smiled. "Thanks, Elijah."

"I value your input."

She laughed. *"Value my input?* Where'd you get that crazy phrase?"

I grinned. "That's what Mom says the president of the PTO says to the parents when they disagree over things."

"I bet they say that when somebody has a stupid idea, and they don't know how to shut 'em up."

Reece gets to the root of things.

"I really mean it," I said. "See you in English."

At lunch Robbie and I sat in the cafeteria and talked in code.

We have to be in "second lunch," which is just a nicey-nice name for: all-the-pizza-and-cookies-are-gone-but-we-still-have-plenty-of-things-like-creamed-corn-and-shepherd's-pie. (The eighth grade pretty much believes that shepherd's pie is either made out of old shepherds, or what old shepherds scrape off their shoes.) The senior highers who have cars skip second lunch and drive to the Whippy Dip for its famous cheeseburgers and raspberry milkshakes.

Over stiff veal parmesan and cold succotash that day, Robbie and I decided our options about the mystery were to *spill* (tell the police), *talk* (tell our parents) or *dig* (check out the grave ourselves). We couldn't spill without talking first, or our parents would explode. So that narrowed our choices to talk or dig. Robbie was for talking. I was for digging. Despite how things looked, I had a nagging feeling in the back of my mind that things weren't what they seemed. Or maybe I just couldn't get my mind around a murder at Camp Mudj. My camp. My home!

"Why would he bury a whole body in a church basement, then move part of it to a cemetery?" I asked. "It's loons."

"Maybe he could only carry parts at a time. And maybe he's moving it because he knows we were there. He's hiding the evidence."

"But why only a few feet away, in a fresh grave that would be easy to find?"

He didn't have an answer.

I don't mind saying I wasn't crazy about getting cornered in that dark hole under the church again. So we worked out a compromise. We'd start digging in the cemetery—better for quick getaway. We'd dig only until we found the sack, no deeper, and decide what to do after that.

"If it is a body," I said, "there'll be evidence on the sack: blood or hair. We can tell the police we saw the old man and thought he was burying treasure. It's a good 'kid answer.' We won't get into trouble."

Robbie was satisfied. Next we had to convince the girls that we should dig. After science, I followed Reece to homeroom. We sat in the back, next to the window.

"It's not exactly true," Reece said, referring to what Robbie and I planned on telling the police if we found a body.

"It's half true."

"Hidden in half-truths are full-blown lies," she said in a preachy tone.

"Is that in the Bible or something?" I snapped.

She made a deadpan face, as if I was an idiot.

"We'll just dig down to the sack, no farther," I said.

"It's evidence."

"Not if there's no crime."

I was right and she knew it. Really, honestly, if I had thought we had a real murder on our hands, I would have told Dad. The last thing I'd want was Camp Mudj in the headlines and me on the front page of the paper. Mom would be the first to serve me a sentence—probably baby-sitting my six-year-old twin sisters, Nori and Stacy, twenty years to life.

Reece thought about what I suggested and stared out the window, her eyes darting across the school yard, looking at nothing. Her eyes looked extra light blue and she seemed pale. She was probably in pain.

"I want to be there," she said finally. Then we had to shut up because there were announcements coming over the PA.

I was glad she wanted to be a part of my plan. But . . . what if we had to make a quick getaway? What if the man should come while we're digging, start shooting at us, or something? How could I . . .

As the announcements rambled on, she slipped me a note: *I know you think I'll just slow you down.* She'd read my mind.

This was the jam I always got in with Reece. She was a good friend and not giggly and dumb like most other girls. She was interested in Indians too. Pretty much everyone liked her, but no one hung around her much because she couldn't keep up. Some days she'd be fine and others she'd be on crutches. It was hard to know how to treat her. I'd seen adults talk almost baby talk to her when she was on crutches, like having weak bones made you dumb.

Ever since Reece and I became project partners last year and won the regional science fair, we'd stayed friends.

I studied her note a minute and wrote back: *You and Mei can be our lookouts, okay? We'll use Dad's walkie-talkies. They reach as far as the cemetery. You can watch from the lodge and hear what's happening. If something goes wrong, you'll be first to know.*

This idea she liked. She whispered. "And a phone's nearby. In case."

The bell rang, and we gathered our books. "Exactly," I said. "And if something happens, you're safe."

"What about you?" she asked with worry in her voice.

"He couldn't catch me. I'm fast enough to—" There I went again, bragging. "I . . . I'm fine. I'll be fine."

"It's all right, Elijah. I know I can't run. It's a great idea about the walkie-talkies. We'll do it that way. You're a genius."

Chapter 5

ROBBIE stayed after school to run lines for the play. It was raining out, but I walked home instead of taking the bus so I could clear my head. The afternoon rain darkened the colors of the leaves to deep green and amber and rust. A few cars swished by on the wet street. The air smelled of earth and leaves. Even in town you're never far from nature. Cut from east to west by one main drag with a few blocks of businesses, Magdeline, Ohio, is lopsided: most of the homes are on the south side. On the north, a couple of little alleys lead down behind the businesses to parking lots, but there's not much else in the way of civilization except for camp and the Morgan farm.

Lots of kids in Magdeline wished they lived in a big city, with movie theaters, fancy restaurants, sports arenas, and malls. They have a point. In the restaurant department, we only have the Whippy Dip, two pizza places, and Florence's—also known as The Greasy Cup, because the coffee comes with a free oil slick on it—where no one under eighteen would be caught dead. We have a drive-in theater, one of the few left in the state, but it's closed half the time. If you need clothes, there's just one sad little department store and a Family Bargain Mart down the road in a shopping center not worth diddly-squat. For sports there's just school football, basketball, and some summer leagues. What you see is what you get.

So Magdeline's not the greatest. But I have to tell you, living at a camp has just about every advantage in the world: a log house to live in with a loft and fireplace; the A-frame lodge and cafeteria with an even bigger fireplace; the lake, the pool, the ropes course and trails; a real lagoon and wildflower meadow; our nature center is home to snakes and lizards. And working for my dad is the best.

The disadvantages are the regular truckloads of little kids running around and Dad being on call twenty-four hours a day. Sometimes the phone will ring at midnight, or later, the nurse reporting some kid with screaming nightmares or appendicitis. Or a raccoon topples a trash can at 3:00 in the morning and scares a bunch of little girls. Or a sewage pipe busts and leaks all over the camp. When Dad's out till daybreak, Mom gets upset and tells him to hire more help. He'll say we can't afford it, and they'll get into a tiff.

I was thinking about all the fall activities—hayrides and hot dog roasts, and planning for Halloween: the "Spiders, Bats, and Other Creepy Things Week," and how the play was pressing down on me, not to mention that I potentially had a slasher murder on my hands. I was on the front porch of my house before I realized the walk home hadn't moved me one step closer to peace of mind.

I do my best brainwork when I become Indian. So, with my bow and arrows and canteen, I set out for Owl Woods, thick and quiet, with a stream running through it all the way to Telanoo. Robbie and I used to climb with binoculars and sandwiches to the top of the biggest chinquapin, which we named Great Oak. Swaying in the breeze in the thin top branches, we could see foxes, squirrels, chipmunks, deer, wild turkey, and a slew of small birds. The high places of the camp are visible from there: the lodge roof and my front porch, also the Morgan barn, and even some rooftops from town.

Dad always takes the all-night campers into the woods. He can do owl calls and the owls actually come, which is very cool. I never get tired of seeing a great horned swooshing through the trees with its huge head and wide wings coming right at us.

Beyond the farthest end of Owl Woods, beyond Great Oak, is where I do my serious thinking, at a place that even Robbie doesn't know about: a thick clump of evergreens I named The Cedars. Indians attach importance to cedars, or so I've read. It smells nice, it's quiet in there, and you're completely hidden. The ground is covered with soft needles—it's perfect for small fires and comfortable sleeping. When the wind comes through, you can hardly feel it, but you can hear it: like putting a seashell to your ear, but better. Close your eyes and hear the ocean roar all around you, even above your head.

Maybe Indians like cedars for the same reasons.

I put down my gear and found a dry spot to sit against a tree trunk. I closed my eyes, breathing in mellow cedar and the earthy smell of dying leaves. I stretched out my legs. It was good to be alone and secret and safe. I would listen, and The Cedars would tell me the right thing to do about the severed head and arm.

When I got back to the school auditorium, work on the play was in full swing. Mei was painting sets. Miss Flewharty, the director, was pushing Reece and Robbie around on the stage. They had lead roles: Reece was Becky Thatcher, Tom Sawyer's girlfriend, and Robbie was Sid, his pesky half-brother. I jumped into helping the construction dads hang the lights and the main backdrop, a huge cloth scrim of green hills and blue sky and clouds. Some of the parents really got into working on the junior high production, even taking time off to help out. The office-type dads loved the manly work, stuff they didn't usually do at home: hammering and sawing and hauling. The set didn't have to be all that good either. Minutes after closing curtain, it'd be in the dumpster.

Dad's canvas came in handy. The construction dads made wood frames and nailed it on, making flats, which Mei painted for the interior scenes, like Aunt Polly's kitchen. A lumber company donated some old planks for the famous whitewashed fence scene.

When most of the cast and crew had gone home, the four of us met backstage. In less than a minute we got into an argument over the digging. Reece had second thoughts. She was still afraid Robbie and I would get shot or something. She came back to the idea of calling the police, or at least telling an adult, or at the very least digging during the day. Mei agreed with everything Reece said. Robbie was just about to jump ship too.

I stood my ground. My original idea still seemed best to me. But had I known what was about to happen, I might have agreed with Reece and saved everyone in Camp Mudj a huge fright.

There was an overnighter going on, and I knew the drill: the campers would be in the dining hall until 6:00; then to a scavenger hunt down by the lake; into Owl Woods from 8:00 to 9:00 for a lesson on nocturnal animals; then back out to the lake for s'mores and songs around the campfire before bunk-time. Robbie and I had roughly an hour—from 8:00 until 9:00—to dig a few feet down and get the sack. Easy enough.

We'd managed to haul our gear around back of the lodge and into the cemetery without being seen. We had a shovel, a walkie-talkie, two flashlights, and rubber gloves—we didn't want to leave fingerprints on the severed head. But finding the actual site took longer than we thought. Everywhere we stepped, our feet sunk into humps of loose, crumbly dirt. I knew they were molehills, but told Robbie in my creepiest voice that dead people had probably been clawing their way out of the ground. He told me to shut up like he halfway believed me.

I thought we'd never find the grave.

Chapter 5

"We're here," I finally whispered into the walkie-talkie. The girls had been dropped off by Reece's mom and were staked out in my room. The lodge was too busy for a stakeout, so they were to tell Mom we were testing the walkie-talkies, if she came home early from her night class in landscaping.

"The grave wasn't in the cemetery," I told Reece and Mei. "It's just outside in another little marked-off place next to one lone tombstone with no writing on it that I can see. It's like a reject grave."

Over the airwaves Reece said, "It's a good thing the place isn't in the graveyard, because you know what just struck me?"

"What? Over," I said.

"It's illegal to dig up someone's grave."

"Oh. Yeah. Okay. Well, the fresh hole is beside the reject grave. So, um . . . roger, over and out."

"Watch your time," said Reece. "Over and out."

The hole was small, maybe two feet square. We got busy, me digging, Robbie holding the light and keeping watch for little flashlight beams to come dancing out of Owl Woods, a sign that the campers were coming down to the lake.

I worked fast as I could. The ground moved pretty easy. When I started huffing and puffing, Robbie offered to take over. I said no. I felt like we were close, and I didn't want him freaking out if he hit something gross. Sure enough, in another minute or so, my shovel sliced through damp dirt cleanly and hit something soft, but resistant.

Deep as the woods are, a big silvery moon on a clear night sheds plenty of light on the path to Owl Woods. A pack of campers were running ahead of the others, without flashlights. We had no warning until we heard a scream. I had just said, "Pay dirt!" knowing I'd hit the sack, when a yelp echoed across the lake, followed by other yelps and full-blown screams. Two things travel well across that lake—sound and light. We heard the campers just as they saw us. I knew what they thought, seeing two guys hunched over a shovel near a cemetery, outlined in moonlight. From across the lake, we looked to them like the old man did to us—grave diggers, or worse: grave *robbers.*

"Duck!" I said, dropping the shovel, grabbing the flashlight, shoving Robbie to the ground, and flattening myself belly down in fresh dirt all at once.

"They saw us!" Robbie said.

I was on the walkie-talkie. "We've been spotted! We're out of here! Over!"

"Who?" came Reece's voice through the static.

"Campers!"

"Go!" she said.

We had maybe a minute before Dad and Bo, our activities and security director, would be out of the woods and around the lake to investigate. My hand went down into that grave—there was no time for rubber gloves—and clawed at dirt until I felt cloth. I grabbed hold and yanked. Out came a mud-caked sack. I didn't have time to process the idea of Dad catching us at grave-robbing, and not believing our treasure-hunting story which, at this particular moment, sounded pretty lame.

"Stay down!" I barked to Robbie.

We belly-crawled for a few yards until we were beyond the church. Bent low, we dashed across the weedy meadow on the far side of the church property and dove under some low branches at the fence line. There we could see but not *be* seen. I turned to Robbie. "We follow this tree line around the back of the property. Stay in the shadows. We'll get into the woods, circle around, and cut behind the kids. We'll cross the creek to dilute our scent, and make it to Great Oak."

"I can't see!" he wheezed.

"Follow me, do what I tell you, and not even bloodhounds can track us."

Police lights flashed red, a siren wailed. Robbie stayed so close behind me through the thickets of Owl Woods that I kept nicking his shins with my heels. But I knew my way. He didn't. We finally got to Great Oak, scrambled up to the top, and watched from there until the campers had been herded into the lodge and the police lights went off. The uproar had died down when it hit me—Mom.

"Reece!" I spoke into the walkie-talkie. "Are you there?"

"Where are you? The police came!" She was breaking up, and I could barely make out her words.

"I know. We can see 'em from here. Is Mom back?"

"No, but she's supposed to be here any second! The baby-sitter just brought the twins in. Where are you!?"

"Up a tree. We're safe and hidden. If she asks where I am, tell her I'm at Robbie's."

"I'm not lying to your mom! I'll tell her the truth, that we're testing the walkie-talkies."

"Half-truth," I teased. "We'll be there in fifteen minutes! Over and out."

"Wait! What happened?" she asked.

"We have the sack. That's all. Over."

Robbie had caught his second wind. "What about the sack?" he asked. "What do we do with it?"

We had two choices: stuff it in my shirt and try to sneak it into my room, or wedge it into a fork in the branches of Great Oak. I explained the choices, then asked Robbie, "Stuff or wedge?"

"Wedge," he said. "If your mom sees it, it'll be in the garbage."

"Okay." I wanted to turn on the flashlight and inspect the sack for blood and hair, or flecks of gold. But we couldn't afford to have the top of Great Oak lit up like a lighthouse across the top of Owl Woods. One of the campers would catch sight of us from the lodge, start squalling, and the police would be on us like a dragnet. I rolled the sack tight. On our way down the tree, I stuffed it into a fork in one of the middle branches. "I'll run over here and get it before school tomorrow," I said. "We'll keep it in my locker."

"I want to come back with you," Robbie said excitedly. "Can I stay over?"

"Yeah, man." I pressed a friendly fist to his shoulder. It was good to hear him getting into the spirit of the adventure.

As soon as my feet hit ground, I broke into a run, careful not to leave Robbie too far behind, but straining to watch through the trees for the lights of Mom's car pulling into the camp. I stopped once for Robbie to catch up, and punched on the walkie-talkie. "What's the status?"

"Coast is still clear, but hurry, Elijah. Your dad asked where you are. I said, 'Out testing the walkie-talkies.' Over."

"We're at the edge of the woods. Start coming downstairs, but keep talking to me. Over."

"Okay. Come on, Mei," I heard her say.

We kept up the banter until we saw the girls on the front porch.

I made it sound like Robbie and I had been on the north and east sides of camp the whole time, toward the Morgan farm where I'd lost contact with the girls. Dad came out of the house, and I stomped across the yard, acting like I was mad we'd missed the whole thing.

Chapter 6

✖✖

BY the next morning at breakfast, everything had been explained. I said we'd been testing out the walkie-talkies to see how far they'd reach, that the girls had tried to tell us about the big fuss, but that we were out of range in a gully, and they kept breaking up. We didn't know what was going on until we saw the police cars leaving, just as we came out of the woods. Mom and Dad believed me.

But I couldn't help thinking about that Bible verse or whatever it was that Reece had said: hidden in half-truths are full-blown lies. I didn't know anything about grave robbers; that was true. But only sort of true.

We were all around the table—the twins, Robbie, and me. (Robbie had to borrow a shirt for school, because his was caked with dirt where he'd lain on the grave. I said he'd slipped in the gully.)

Stacy plopped a wad of butter on her pancakes and asked, "Did they catch the grave robbers?"

"They weren't grave robbers," Mom answered. "The police concluded they were probably just kids digging for night crawlers, and were scared off by the campers' screams."

"What are night crawlers?" Stacy asked, making a yuck face.

"Big, juicy worms that come slithering out of graves at night!" I said.

"Not at the breakfast table, Elijah!" Mom yelled. Then she turned to the twins and said comfortingly, "They don't come out of graves, girls. Fishermen look for them in good soil because they make very good fishing bait."

"A little late in the year for crawlers," Dad said.

Nori held the syrup high over her bowl and drizzled a long, skinny brown stream on her pancakes. "Look! There's a night crawler in my pancakes."

"That's enough, Nori!" Mom corrected. She gave me the viper look; that's when her head tips down and her forehead juts forward like she's going to strike, and her eyes drill into me until they almost cross. "Now see what you've started, Elijah?"

I'm always getting viped when the twins are around.

Robbie and I didn't have time before school to get the sack. Reece and Mei were waiting at my locker, disappointed that we showed up empty-handed.

"We'll get it," was all I said.

Antsy to get the mysterious grave sack, the four of us fidgeted and drummed our fingers and exchanged impatient looks through every class we shared. If the rest were like me, they were imagining the worst: that a squirrel or a crow would make off with the sack, or that a sudden downpour would wash away all the bloodstains or gold flecks, though there wasn't a cloud in the sky. I was itching to get that sack. But because the girls had been good lookouts, and because I'd promised Reece I'd include her, I rounded up everyone when the bell rang and suggested we all go together. "Call your moms and tell them we're working on the play and we need to go to my house."

Reece gritted her teeth. "I'm not lying to my mom!"

"And we can take the golf cart!" I added.

I'm not old enough to drive, but I am allowed to use the camp's golf cart, to haul gear and take kids with disabilities to the sites.

Reece burst into a big grin. "The golf cart? Awesome!"

Mom made a snack, and we ate out on the porch. The girls sat in the swing and we guys got the wicker chairs from the set on the other end of the porch. Mom hung around and poured juice. We tried to make small talk while we ate, but it was hard. Our minds were elsewhere, but we couldn't talk about *that* because of Mom.

"Reece and Mei have never been into Owl Woods," I told Mom.

"A nice day for a walk," she said to the girls. She gave me a wide-eyed fake smile that said, *Do you know what you're doing? What about . . . her?* Her eyes drifted to Reece, then back to me, then to Reece again.

"We're taking the cart," I answered the goggly way she looked at me, "because . . . um, we all have homework and we don't want to be gone that long."

"Ah, I see," she said and nodded privately to me in approval.

Moms are funny. One minute they put you in charge of the entire world, the next they think you're too stupid to know that your friend—the one who spends half her time on crutches—can't walk across acres of hilly paths.

Reece was onto Mom's goggly look. She turned directly to Mom and smiled sweetly, but there was a definite edge in her voice: "We do have homework, Mrs. Creek, but mostly we have to take the golf cart because I'm crippled, and I can't walk far without keeling over. People are always doing wonderful favors because of my problem and I really appreciate it. But I don't need to be protected from my own life."

It bordered on backtalk, but Mom just turned a little red and nodded, "Oh, yes . . . sure, hon."

If *I* had talked to Mom like that she'd have viped me, then yelled and sent me out to pull weeds for the next hour.

In the dead silence we all had a minute to understand that Reece had faced up to her disability, and she expected everyone around her to do the same. She'd break a few heads, if she had to.

I changed the subject. "Is Dad around?"

"He's in a meeting with the architect about the next phase of the expansion."

"Cool."

We sipped and munched.

Mom stood behind me, fiddling with my hair and patting me on the shoulders. "Well, Mei, I saw you briefly at the house the other night, but with trying to get the girls settled down after all the confusion—those kids in the graveyard . . . Elijah, you haven't formally introduced us."

"Sorry. This is Mei Aizawa. She's from Japan. She and Reece hang out."

"Glad to officially meet you. How long have you been in America?"

"Two years. I like it very much."

More munching.

Robbie said, "Boy, how 'bout that pre-algebra homework?"

We ate fast. As we took our plates inside, Mom tugged at my sleeve. "Drive slow," she whispered, "and you be careful with that little girl. She's delicate."

I rolled my eyes and whispered back, "Only on the outside."

I left a note on the maintenance bulletin board saying I was driving Mei and Reece and Robbie into Owl Woods.

I can't begin to say how I felt when we set out across the camp that sunny fall afternoon. The wind blew as warm as summer, the trees glowed oranges and reds in the afternoon sun, and yellows and greens against the bluest sky I'd ever seen. It was like beginning an adventure, a quest. I drove carefully, weaving along the path through the woods. Reece leaned her head back and closed her eyes and let the wind blow through her long blond hair.

"Watch the road," she said. How she knew I was looking at her I can't guess. Then she said, "Elijah, about your Mom.

Chapter 6

She's really nice, and I didn't mean to be snotty, but if I don't make it plain, people don't get it."

Mei loved the cart. "I never did golf in Japan, but we have many small cars, like this one!" In high spirits, we decided someday we'd all visit Japan. Mei said, "Oh, you must come to my home!" At that moment—me behind the wheel with the trees blazing and the warm wind blowing—it seemed possible.

I got uneasy when the paved path ended and we had to cross a gully and go the rest of the way on foot, because—and this I never told Robbie or anyone, having learned it myself only in the last year from a big map of Camp Mudj—Great Oak was not actually in the camp part of Owl Woods, but in Telanoo. Here we were in the land no one owns with the key to buried treasure. Or murder.

The girls watched from the ground as Robbie and I brought down the sack. We took turns handing it off, using our shirttails because we'd left the rubber gloves down with the girls. Even after our feet hit ground, Reece kept staring up through the huge limbs of Great Oak, resting her hand on its rough bark.

"What can you see from up there?" she asked me.

"Everything," I answered.

We made a circle. Slowly we unrolled the sack, each of us leaning in to be the first to see the blood—or the gold.

The girls turned it over, examined it inside and out. An old,

49

muddy gunnysack, that's all it was, with an old rag inside.

"No blood," I said.

Robbie's shoulders drooped. "No gold."

And no clues about the severed head and arm. Reece dropped the sack; we sat back and heaved sighs of disappointment. That's when Mei reached in once more, to the very bottom of the sack, feeling around, then turning it inside out. There, stuck in the seam, were several tiny rings of wire, all interconnected to make a kind of metal cloth. She held it up with two fingertips. We all closed in around it, studying it in silence for a minute or two.

"What is it?" Robbie asked.

"It's something," I said stupidly, as if *that* were a revelation.

"Mesh," said Reece.

She held out her gloved hand. Mei laid the little piece of wire mesh on Reece's palm. Wadded up, it looked like a tiny pile of sand. When Reece spread it out in the middle of her hand, the whole thing wasn't three inches across.

"It looks old," she said.

Mei studied it. "Jewelry maybe?"

"A woman's jewelry," Robbie suggested.

It hadn't struck me that it might be a *woman's* head and arm in the grave. I looked at Reece and she was thinking the same thing. Maybe the old man had killed his wife.

We went around the circle, giving one theory after another:

Maybe it was his wife's jewelry, and he killed her.

Maybe she just died by accident.

No, because why would he cut up a body?

Maybe he's loons.

Maybe he's a serial killer.

He looks too old and frail.

Maybe he just kills old, frail people.

That's goofy. And buries them in church basements? Come on!

There's only one body; we can't jump to conclusions.

We don't know there even is a body; there's no blood on the sack.

Right. There would have to be blood.

Unless it's an old body.

Then the sack would stink.

Yeah, I think it's a piece of a treasure.

Shaped like a head and arm?

We were back to where we started.

I was thinking we had to find out what the mesh meant, when Reece said those very words: "We have to find out what it means."

I smiled at her. She smiled back. "Yeah." She was in it with me, no matter what. In the fall sunshine through gold leaves, she looked really healthy. Her eyes were all sparkly with excitement and adventure. My heart suddenly thumped in my chest.

We knelt there in a huddle, Reece's hand opened out in the middle of us, holding the little piece of mesh, which she kept touching with her fingertip.

Just looking at it gave us a kind of courage. We all sort of glowed.

"It *is* something," I said again, only this time it didn't sound dumb. "The piece of a puzzle. A mystery. Maybe murder, maybe treasure."

"We have to try digging again. At night," Reece said, which surprised me.

"Or dawn," I said. "We'll have enough light to see without flashlights."

"And this time, Elijah, check the camp schedule *and* the cycle of the moon!" Robbie said, jabbing at my shoulder.

I was ready to take a swat at him, when it all came back—us sneaking through the graveyard, sinking in molehills, digging by moonlight, running for our lives from screaming campers, treed like squirrels. It was nothing but funny now.

I sat back and started laughing. Maybe the whole treasure mystery was just too cool for me to hold inside, or maybe it was the hollow thrill of being in forbidden Telanoo, and no one but me aware of it. I laughed until the others thought I was crazy.

"We have no idea what we're getting into," I said, throwing myself back on the ground. Gazing up through the leaves to the blue sky, it seemed like the whole world was opening up. "Is everybody game?"

"I'm game, Elijah," Reece said right away. "Let's seal it."

I sat up. She closed her fingers over the piece of mesh.

I put my hand over hers in the middle of the huddle. Robbie put his hand on mine in agreement. "Game."

Mei looked confused, but laid her hand on top and nodded. "Game."

THE girls came over the night before the dig. I made it look businesslike. Mei and I talked about backdrops and costumes. Reece and Robbie memorized lines. Then we had popcorn and Mei made origami animals for the twins. Around 10:00 we started watching an old *Tom Sawyer* movie for research. Robbie and I caught the adventure bug and decided to play like Tom Sawyer and camp out in the Tree House Village. Reece was tired, so she and Mei went off to the guest room, but not before we made a deal. They were to sneak out and meet us before 6:00. If they got caught, they'd say they were coming down to scare us awake. Which could be the truth.

After the movie Mom dug out the winter sleeping bags. She whispered that it was gallant of me to be so nice to a girl with a disability and an international student. "You're a good citizen," she gushed as she gave Robbie and me a thermos of hot chocolate and sent us off into the frosty dark.

Dad was building Camp Mudjokivi in stages, and the past summer had been dedicated to getting the tree houses started. It was going to be the coolest: cabins on stilts in a cluster, each connected by rope bridges with a meeting room in the middle. The village was tucked into the woods, so you'd feel like you really lived up in a tree. The platforms were done and the rope bridges too. We camped on the central meeting room floor, which had a roof over it, and talked about the severed head and arm until every sound from the woods seemed like a footstep. It was hard to sleep.

The sky was all red and purple that Saturday when the four of us—dressed in dark clothes and outfitted with penlights, a shovel, and a garden trowel—crept around Old Pilgrim Church and picked our way through the tombstones and molehills to the far side. Everybody at Camp Mudj was still asleep. Predawn would give us a better shot at avoiding suspicion . . . or coming face-to-face with the old man creeping around. The girls stood watch for good measure.

I was beginning to think that, for some mysterious reason, things go better with the girls involved. Mom seemed to immediately trust me more just because Reece and Mei were around. Mostly girls are too scared or giggly to do things, but Reece was different. And Mei hardly ever said a word without getting majority approval, so she was easy to have along—and much smarter than she let on: straight As to my Bs, even though she's not great with English.

Robbie and I took turns digging. About three feet down Robbie hit something. The shovel went *clank*—as if on metal—and he was up out of that hole like he'd struck a nest of tarantulas.

The sun was almost up, which meant the linen truck would be delivering towels to the lodge. I told everyone to stay low. I grabbed the garden trowel and dropped down in the hole. In archaeologist fashion, I carefully scraped aside handfuls of dirt. Though I'd braced myself for anything, even dead eyes looking up at me, I still jumped back and gasped when I scraped back a layer of dirt and two empty sockets appeared.

The others gasped too, and for a minute we froze, staring at the empty eyes of a dirt-smeared, severed head.

It wasn't bone, but metal, and not a skull . . . a helmet. *A treasure!* Wild with relief and excitement, I shoved my fingers under the nosepiece and lifted carefully. It was kind of medieval, or Roman maybe, and battered. It had a gold tint and mysterious symbols carved into the forehead and all around.

Robbie, who I'm sure had expected to see a rotting face and throw up on it, leaned over the hole with such enthusiasm he almost toppled in. "The arm! Get the arm!" he said.

"I'm getting it! Girls, keep watch! We're almost done."

Hesitantly I handed over the helmet to Robbie, barely able to let go. I could hardly take my eyes off it.

Dirt flew everywhere as I shoveled deeper, to the left, to the right. The red sun had just popped over the trees. Dad would be out and about soon. My shovel jammed against something soft, which turned out to be wire mesh, like the scrap that had gotten caught on the burlap sack. I carefully eased it out of the dirt. It was the arm, or rather an arm piece from a suit of armor, solid at the shoulder and forearm with mesh in between, and what was left of a leather glove.

"Chain mail," Robbie said mysteriously. Reece and Mei took their eyes off the camp for a second to give the arm a closer glance.

We'd planned our strategies the night before: if it was a body, we were going straight to Dad to tell him we'd been digging for night crawlers where the "grave robbers" had, and stumbled on a corpse. If we found anything else, it was to be our secret, until a unanimous vote said otherwise.

We'd brought the sack and the rag and the piece of wire mesh, so we'd have everything all together, in case this was a crime scene.

We stuffed the pieces in the sack. I jumped out of the hole, and all of us hurriedly shoved dirt until it looked pretty much like before. "Okay," I said. "Robbie, take these to Great Oak and wait for us there. I'll go back to the Tree House Village and get the sleeping bags. You girls go raid the refrigerator at the lodge. Here's the key. We don't want to risk getting the third degree from Mom at the house. Don't give me that look, Reece, it's allowed. I work here a lot, you know. It's not stealing. I'll meet you around back with the golf cart. "Okay, let's go!"

Reece and Mei and I could hardly contain our excitement on our way back through the cemetery.

"It is a treasure?" Mei asked.

"A mysterious treasure," Reece whispered. "But why would an old man bury pieces of armor in a graveyard?"

"Outside a graveyard," I corrected. "And why bury it in the church crawl space first?" I asked. "And is the rest of it still there? That's the next question."

I wanted to break into the basement right then—and probably would have, just to see what was really buried under that human-shaped mound behind the plank door—except Reece and Mei would have gone into fits. And, yeah, I wouldn't want Robbie hanging around in the woods forever, hungry for breakfast with the treasure all to himself. Just holding the helmet in my hands for a minute, there'd been a kind of tingling up my arms. It occurred to me that Robbie shouldn't rub the symbols or try to read them or chant them or anything. Who knew what kind of strange power the words might have? I imagined getting to Great Oak, only to find the helmet and arm lying near the tree trunk, with a sad little Robbie-looking toad nearby crying *ribbit-ribbit*.

The morning air was crisp and the sky like Indian turquoise. As we crossed the wooden bridge over Rocky Creek, it seemed to me again like we were heading into a different life.

We sat under Great Oak in a tight circle with the burlap in the middle of us again, but now it held the helmet and arm piece. Reece had the scrap of chain mail nestled in the rag at her feet. Mei suggested we dust ourselves off and wash our hands with the canteen water. Good call. She had brought a tiny little notebook and mini colored pencils. She took notes and made some sketches, stopping every few minutes to look at the helmet, shake her head and whisper, *"Sugoi . . ."* which Reece translated "wow." We felt like archaeologists, elbow deep in an expedition.

The helmet was hard to describe. Robbie, the history buff, couldn't nail it down to a certain time period. "This is mysterious," he said. "Really mysterious."

In one way it was plain: a simple shape, with no big showy points or blades or plumes coming out of the top, like you'd see in old movies about ancient Rome. But it seemed to be made of several kinds of metal. The main part was a tan-gold metal, like bronze. Six strips of dark gray—designed to protect the soldier's head from club or sword—met at the top and curved down to meet a band that circled the head. Narrow lines etched into the metal arched around the helmet and connected every other end of the steel-looking cross braces, so that when you looked at the helmet from the top, it made a kind of flower or star design.

The band was pale gold and silver-colored, engraved with vines and leaves. Short spikes stuck out in different directions from the band. At the end of some of the spikes were little knobs, or rivets, of copper.

Reece was first to notice that the copper was still reddish and not blue-green like copper turns when it tarnishes. We couldn't figure why that was so, if the helmet was so old. The nosepiece came down narrow but heavy between the eyes and ended in a triangle. The sides and back of the helmet came down to protect the neck. It wasn't the kind of helmet that covered the whole face, the kind that looked like it would smother you, but an open type. Strange letters were engraved between the eyeholes.

It had been lined with leather, which had probably connected to a chinstrap, but most of the lining had rotted away.

The arm piece had a solid metal shoulder and forearm mounted on a sleeve of the chain mail, and a leather glove. A mysterious word engraved on the forearm was the same type of alphabet as the word on the helmet.

Reece looked long and hard at the words.

"What is it?" Robbie asked.

She stared way off as if she had some wild idea, her eyes intense and darting around in deep thought. Then she looked at the word again, then off into nowhere again. You could practically hear the gears in her brain grinding.

"What?!" I demanded.

"If this was English, how would you pronounce it?" she asked.

"I don't know . . . koiv-wa-via?" I said.

"Or kolv-wa-via," Robbie offered. "The third letter looks more like an *L*. Sort of looks Russian to me."

Mei shook her head. "Not Russian."

Reece's mouth dropped open. She knew something.

"What?!" I cried again.

"Could it be . . . Greek?" Reece asked.

"Greek?" Mei asked thoughtfully, and started to nod.

"Greek, maybe . . . I have been to a Greek restaurant—Kavouris, New York City. Letters like that. Yes."

Reece got the weirdest look: part fear, part excitement, with puzzlement and hope and uncertainty all mixed in.

"Will you please spill whatever you're thinking?" I said again.

"I'm not sure! But . . ." She touched the word on the helmet, "but . . . I think I have to bring someone else in."

"No!" Robbie cried. "It's a secret! You promised! No one else can share the treasure!"

"Reece, no," I said evenly. "We made a pact."

"But we need an expert."

"No adults!" Robbie cried.

"Oh, he's one of us," she said cryptically. "We can trust him."

Mei leaned in. "Who, Reece?"

"The only kid I know who might understand what this means."

Chapter 8

I moved my desk in front of my bedroom window so I could do homework and keep half an eye on the church and the edge of the cemetery.

On Monday morning Reece and I had a stare-down at her locker. Her eyes begged at me. We had to get a second opinion about the helmet sooner or later, she said. True, but I still didn't like the idea. It was hard to say no to her. Robbie showed up and had the idea to copy the letters off on paper and have the "expert" decipher them. But for reasons she wouldn't explain, Reece insisted the expert had to see the pieces. She argued again that he was just like us and would swear to secrecy. Then Mei showed up. The four of us were deadlocked. Reece wouldn't break her promise about keeping our secret, but she wouldn't budge about wanting this person in. I had a sneaking suspicion she already *had* been talking to whoever it was.

Robbie agreed with me. Mei refused to have an opinion but nodded at everything Reece said. I called for a powwow at camp when the coast cleared.

A lot was going on at Camp Mudj with a Ladies Fall Craft Fair and a Sleepaway Weekend coming up: seventy third-graders from Cleveland schools. I knew from experience that at all hours of the weekend, parents would be driving in to get their whiny, homesick city kids. I personally think Sleepaway Weekend is a bad idea and have told Dad so, but he says we need to take every group that will book us to "stay afloat." Mom calls it Sleepless Weekend. She turns into a grouch and I have to watch the twins while she goes out to drink coffee with her friends.

Play rehearsals were in full swing, but I was determined to get back into the church before the powwow, to get the rest of what was buried in the crawl space—by myself, if necessary.

Then, one night at dinner I heard faint hammering echo across the camp. No one else in my family heard it. It was too late for staff to be working on the Tree House Village. I excused myself, ran to my room, and looked out the window. Somebody had just boarded up the windows and doors of Old Pilgrim Church!

The old man! I hissed to myself. *Drats!*

I ran to the lodge, cut through the assembly room, and pressed my face to the back window for a better look at the church. Sure enough—it was nailed tight. *Rotten luck!* I stomped around the lodge for a good minute, not caring if anyone came in and saw my tirade. I even surprised myself at how miffed I was. *We waited too long! Getting the rest of the treasure is going to be harder now!*

I cooled off and tried to look on the bright side. My guess was he'd closed up the church to protect his secret. The basement grave had been shaped like a whole man, proof enough to me that there had to be more there, probably a whole suit of armor. *Well,* I said to myself, peering out the window again, *at least it's safe. At least it's close by.*

Did he know we'd dug up the helmet and arm piece, which were now hanging in a plastic bag in the upper branches of Great Oak? I hoped like everything that he didn't. I called everyone with an update. Reece pressed me about her expert. In the end I caved. But I decided to plan an initiation at the powwow. I wasn't going to make this easy.

Reece's expert turned out to be Marcus Skidmore, aka Skid. He was pretty new to Magdeline. At our first class meeting last year, he'd stood up and greeted everyone and described himself as half white, half black, and half Latino. Which of course meant he was a hundred and fifty percent of a person, while the rest of us were only a hundred percent. I knew right away he had a big ego. The girls all thought he had a kind of mystique because he was dark skinned like a black person, but with short wavy hair and light green eyes. He was an army brat and had lived all over the world. Skid was always using foreign words and flashing around photos of himself standing in front of the Louvre in Paris and the Coliseum in Rome and the Great Wall of China. He must have been a real annoyance for show-and-tell in preschool.

If I'd known Skid was Reece's expert, I never would have agreed to it. I was especially miffed when she invited him to the powwow before I'd told the others about my decision, before we could plan his initiation trials.

I situated us on the far side of the lake near the trees, which sort of shielded us from the rest of the camp. I built a small fire to take the chill off the late afternoon. The meeting was just underway when—and this was the icing on the cake, as far as I was concerned—Skid made his grand entrance by whizzing in on his skateboard, all the way down the lake path. He was wearing dark jeans and a jacket, a black T-shirt and high-tops—fake-looking street gang getup.

Mei and Reece thought his entrance was just super. Robbie and I rolled our eyes at each other. *That's all we need,* I grumbled to myself, *a show-off, when our secret treasure has to be kept under wraps!* Reece already had sworn him to secrecy, but I made him swear again.

I tossed around some bags of chips and made small talk about the camp just to make him wait, test him out.

As the sun sank behind the trees, Robbie reluctantly pulled the helmet and arm piece out of the sack, and I don't mind saying I was shocked at how quick that suave, world traveler Marcus Skidmore lost his cool.

"Whoa . . . wow . . . oh wow, Reece," he whispered, kneeling to touch the pieces reverently. I made him put on rubber gloves. He rubbed his hand over the letters on the helmet like it was a crystal ball. He looked at Reece and smiled. "You were right. It's ancient Greek."

How does Reece know ancient Greek?

We all closed in around the circle. I kept an eye out for camp staff.

"Is the helmet old?" Robbie asked excitedly.

"I don't know, but the words are," Skid said.

"You don't know?!" I carped. "I thought you were the expert!"

Reece showed him the scrap of mesh wrapped in the piece of rag. "Can we have this dated?"

"Possibly," Skid said. He studied the intertwined rings for a minute, then wrapped it up in the rag and put it in his pocket.

"Where are you taking that?" I asked. I could just see him forgetting he had it and blowing his nose on that rag and ruining good evidence.

"I'm going to Chicago with my dad next weekend. He knows a scientist there."

"You can't tell your dad!" Robbie cried.

"I'm not telling anyone anything," Skid said shortly. "But we need answers, like how old is the armor? What's it made from? Where's the rest of it?"

"Proceed with caution," Mei said, quoting a road sign she'd seen, I guess.

Reece agreed. "We have to move quickly, but carefully. And we have to trust each other." Her eyes slid over to me.

Skid pulled a huge book out of his backpack and began flipping through it, but his words were directed at me. "I don't want a cut of the treasure money, if that's what anyone's thinking."

I struck a casual pose. "I didn't say anything."

He gave me a dry look, then went back to his book, a Greek lexicon, and within a minute he'd found both words: "The word on the helmet—*soterion*—means 'salvation.' On the arm piece . . . *koinonia* means 'fellowship.'" He showed us the pages.

I was a little disappointed with the translation. In the back of my mind, I'd hoped for a real zinger like "Millennium Key" or "Dark Knight" or "Curse of Death." I threw another log on the fire and sent Robbie and Mei to get sticks to roast hot dogs.

"What's the significance of that?" I asked, but Reece and Skid were head-to-head, studying the decorations and markings. "And why Greek?" I mumbled. "Does that mean the armor is Greek? Doesn't look Greek to me." I might as well have been a cricket for all the attention they paid to my questions. I kept myself company doing owl calls while I stoked the fire.

" . . . and the rest of it may be in the church up there," she told him quietly.

Skid eyed the boarded-up church on the ridge behind the Virginia creeper hedge. "How do we get in?"

"We broke in the first time," Reece answered.

I objected, "We did not, but we'll do it again if we have to, and only if I say so."

I knew right away that made no sense, so I covered with, "The group decides everything. Four votes."

He smirked. "So . . . only if you say so. The church belongs to you, I guess."

"No, but it borders my camp."

"*Your* camp?" Skid said, leveling his eyes at me. "I'm impressed. Quite the businessman you are." He looked around and nodded. "Quite a spread. What's the name again—Camp Mud-in-your-skivvies?"

Reece burst into giggles.

"Cute," I said, being a good sport. But I couldn't keep the smile going for long.

Robbie and Mei came back with sticks and started the hot dogs. Reece came around the fire to me. She put a hand on my arm to steady herself. "Elijah, don't be mad. We're in this together."

"I'm fine," I said.

"You don't look fine."

"Well, I am fine!" I insisted.

A few days ago I had reassured her that she'd be included in our quest. Suddenly it felt like the tables were turned. Now it was me on the fringe, her telling me that she and Skid wouldn't leave me out.

I can't even describe how that tore me up inside.

"He's here to help us." She squeezed my arm and smiled. "We're going to solve it, Elijah, and it may be a much greater treasure than we first thought."

I had defrosted my attitude a little by the time the food was ready. There's nothing that helps the world make sense like wolfing down a three-fourths-charred hot dog with mustard and a mug of hot cider while crickets chirp and fire crackles and night clouds float past the moon. We stashed the armor pieces behind the trees in case anyone like Dad or Bo came upon us in the dark. The fire was down to coals, and the sun had gone down a half hour ago; we huddled closer and decided to get back into the church, but only if it didn't involve breaking glass or any kind of vandalism. Reece insisted. *Drat that old man with his hammer and pocket full of nails! He made a mountain of work out of a molehill. Doggone him!*

The other three took turns telling Skid how they'd seen the old man burying what we thought was a severed head, how the mists had crept up from the lake, how the girls were lookouts with the walkie-talkies. I still wasn't sure he could be trusted. I was steering the conversation to how molehills in a graveyard look like dead people are clawing their way up—all kinds of good scary campfire stuff—when Robbie's face suddenly went slack. He was across the fire from me, facing the woods. I heard a scuffling noise behind me, where the armor pieces were hidden. We hushed. Everyone's eyes turned to the trees behind me. Mei choked back a scream. Nobody offered a clue as to what was happening. From the terror-stricken look on their faces—even Skid's—it took every ounce of willpower I had to turn around and see for myself.

A pair of eyes glowed above the bag of armor pieces. Then two pairs, then four, then more coming out of the darkness, encircling us . . . five pairs of eyes, seven pairs of glowing eyes . . .

Chapter 9

I can't say which idea came into my head first because they were all there at once: that all that touching the helmet and reciting of the words on it had conjured up evil spirits; that stomping through graves then laughing about it had awakened the dead. But one idea stayed because it made the most sense—after I got a grip on myself. I whispered it to the others as I turned ever so slowly back to the fire: "Skunks. Don't move."

I nudged another log into the fire with my toe, hoping the sparks going up would make them back away.

"Stay put," I said quietly. "The heat drew them out. No sudden moves." Figuring the word *skunks* was not in Mei's vocabulary, and seeing the terror in her eyes, I slowly pinched my nose and said, "Smell bad animal." She got it. We just sat there hoping the family of skunks wouldn't leave a deposit on our treasure or worse: on us. It had happened to a camper once before. He was a rotten kid and maybe deserved it. But the stink and the gross tomato juice bath and being dubbed "Reeking Roland" and "Stench Boy" the whole week . . . I wouldn't wish it on a dog.

Robbie ever so gently laid a paper bag and some napkins on the fire. Flames flared. The skunks backed away and ambled off into the dark, leaving a souvenir in the air around us. After that the powwow was pretty much over.

Mom smelled me coming and wouldn't let me inside the house until she'd tossed out a robe and made me change behind a bush. When I got into the kitchen, there on the table was a large can of tomato juice, with instructions.

In my room that night, propped up in bed in the quiet dark, with my eyes on the old church and my mind on the powwow, I understood why it bothered me so much that Skid was now in the mix. As I said before, I may be part Creek Indian. So I've done a little study of their ways. They come from a larger group called the Muskogees, who lay claim to the power of the Sacred Fire. People who come together to dance or sing or whatever are people of the same fire, a clan. I just wasn't sure Skid was of the same fire as Robbie, Reece, Mei, and me. As different as the four of us were, we fit together good.

But there was something else too: the legend of the Four Teachers, the People of the Light. No one knows where they came from, but it's said that the first came from the north, the second from the east, the third from the south, and the fourth from the west. The Four Teachers brought the medicine ways to the Indians—arts of healing with nature and ceremonies to keep themselves wise and powerful.

Maybe, in the back of my mind, I believed that four was the best number, like a number of power.

But there were five of us now, and we didn't dance or sing around the fire that night. We almost got into a tiff over the armor, ate too many hot dogs, and came away smelling like Stench Boy.

"There is a connection! I believe it," Reece whispered to Skid in pre-algebra the next day. His head bobbed in agreement. The two of them had come up with this wild tale that the dismembered armor had something to do with the closing of Old Pilgrim Church. I could not have cared less about that. The old church had been standing there rotting for as long as I'd been alive and obviously a lot longer. But when I overheard the words *ancient warfare* and *demonic powers,* I perked up. Just as I asked what they were talking about, Mr. Ridenour started handing out the quiz, and for the next hour we were plunged into the cold, murky waters of pre-algebra. (Which I'd already figured out was just plain algebra. They were just trying to sneak the hard stuff in on us a year early.)

Over the next week—while Skid was waiting for the test results from his scientist friend on the piece of mesh, and while the other four of us were approaching the final rehearsals of *Tom Sawyer*—I lost interest in their mumbo jumbo. Personally, I came to believe that, if we could find the rest of the old relic, we could get a pretty penny for it. Robbie was half hoping it wasn't worth anything so he could have it for the school's costume closet, and be the first one to wear it if they ever did *King Arthur.* Mei thought we should turn it over to authorities or to a museum. As she put it, "American children act very independent of the families. Not good."

But something boiled up in me the day I found Reece and Skid sitting close in study hall, swapping secrets. I went over and dumped my backpack on their table.

"What's up?" I said as cool as I could, pulling out a chair.

"Hey, Creek, have a seat."

I plopped down. "I got one already."

Reece leaned across the table. I got a whiff of strawberry shampoo. "Elijah, we were just talking about the—you know, and we were wondering about the best place to keep it. Somewhere we all could get at it easily to study it. But someplace safe."

"The safest place is where it is now," I grumped. "Great Oak."

"But, Elijah, the rest of us . . . well, it's so far from the rest of us."

"You got a better idea?" I eyed Skid coldly.

He was leaning back, his arm laid around the back of Reece's chair. For the life of me, I couldn't stop the slow burn creeping up my face.

He started a list, with reasons for each one. Under his bed. Because, except for a step-brother in another state, Skid was an only child. He had no little kids at home to snoop around like I had. Or the storage closet in his condo, which was always under lock and key. Or a secret stashing place in the ceiling of his closet. Reece nodded at every suggestion. He started to go on. I stood.

Reece said, "I'd keep it myself, Elijah, but there's no place at my apartment. Mom would find it for sure. Skid just thought—"

"I have to get to class," I said, scooping up my books.

I skulked off with echoes in my head: *Skid said, Skid just thought, Skid this, Skid that. He was a worm, worming his way in, smooth and slimy, taking over the whole operation.* "Snake!" I fumed under my breath. "Night crawler!"

I needed to think. So . . . rain, snow, or sleet—didn't matter—tonight I'd be at The Cedars. They were calling me.

Skid appeared at the front door of my house a half hour after I got back from play rehearsal.

"I just got a call," he said. "He wants to know where we got it."

I looked at him through the screen. His skateboard was lying out in the yard. He always wore dark colors, which made his dark skin even darker and his light eyes even lighter and a little strange. "Who?" I asked.

"Dr. Stallard," he said coolly. "He called from Chicago."

"It's none of his business," I growled. My head shot around to make sure the twins weren't nearby. I stepped out onto the porch and pulled the door shut. The screen slammed behind me.

"I know that, Creek" he said. "But the truth is we're going to have trouble keeping this quiet."

"Oh, that's a news flash!" I said sarcastically. "See, that's why I didn't want you flying off to Chicago with—"

"It's a thousand years old," he said matter-of-factly.

I was speechless. There was a gleam of satisfaction in his eyes.

"'Roughly' is what Dr. Stallard said, roughly eight hundred to a thousand years old. He knew it was chain mail. And here's what I told him . . ." Skid's eyebrows went up and his voice got a snooty, parental tone, "I told him that it was secret where we got it, and that it was *in good hands.* He's just worried that we'll ruin the piece, you know, wash all the clues off or lose it or break it. He gave me instructions on how to keep the rest of it safe. He knows we have an archaeological find, that's all. He promised to help."

I didn't trust Skid, but what he said was making some sense. "Well, as long as you keep checking back with me before you talk with him. Every time. And as long as he won't follow you here."

Skid laughed. "He's in Chicago."

"How can you be sure?" I defended.

Skid shoved his hands into his pockets and got quiet. He looked down at the porch floor a minute, then shifted his weight toward me as if to tell a secret, eyes still down. "Listen, Elijah. I'm not the enemy. I keep my word. You can count on that. I make no claim on the helmet, or the arm piece." Then he looked up and his green eyes drilled into me. "Or Reece."

I wanted to slug him. I wanted to say, "Shut up! She has nothing to do with anything!" But that would have looked like I really did like Reece and was embarrassed to have anyone know it.

He extended his hand for me to shake. "We're on the same side. Deal?"

I hated him and admired him all at the same time, acting like a big shot, trying to smooth things out and be mature, making me feel like a kid. If only I had extended my hand first. If only I'd said something right back about Reece like, "Reece and I've been friends for over a year and nothing or no one will ever change that."

Instead I got hot behind the eyeballs.

"Deal. Sure," I said. "Just be careful, that's all I'm saying."

I shook hands, kind of grudgingly.

"We have the same goal," he said. "We both want to find out the truth."

"I'm curious, though," I said coolly. "Why did you have to see it for yourself? Why couldn't you just translate the words?"

"The words are only part of the puzzle. Reece thinks the symbols could have deep meaning." He didn't really answer the question.

"Well, Skid, you've got your mysterious symbols and deep meaning and all that rot—and then there's the question of big money." I grinned knowingly. "The helmet may be worth a fortune."

His eyes narrowed at me.

"Hey," I defended, *"I'm* not sending it off to the highest bidder. I wouldn't do that. The group decides everything. I'm just saying . . ." I trailed off.

He knew I had sway over the others and that, if I pressed

hard enough, they'd probably go with whatever I decided, no matter what he and his Dr. Stallard said.

"I gotta go in," I said. "You keep everything under wraps until I say so." As the screen slammed behind me, I felt his eyes still drilling into me. What was his problem anyway?

I went to the living room window and watched him sail out the driveway to the entrance road. Smooth and swift, he disappeared into the darkness like a snake.

A few things about Marcus Skidmore: he'd never cheated on a test that I'd seen or heard of, and he didn't lie to the teachers. And though he didn't play up to them like some kids, he was one of their favorites. Whether they liked him because he was one of the few ethnic kids in our school and they were taking care not to discriminate, or because his street gang look made him a little scary and teachers wanted to stay on his good side, I couldn't figure. He'd probably be picked Student of the Year. But the thing was, he didn't do the usual Student of the Year stuff: no save-the-children food drives, or top test scores or extra credit projects, no fancy Christmas presents for all the teachers. He wasn't all that impressive. (Okay, the skateboard stunt down the lake path was sort of spectacular.) Most people thought he was super for no real reason.

Maybe Skid was a con artist and I was the only one in Magdeline who could see it. I hadn't given him the Indian test of character yet, where you close your eyes and listen to a person talk, tuning in for the honesty and integrity in his voice. I tucked that idea in the back of my mind for later and took off for The Cedars.

I sat in the cold, velvety, moonless quiet for a long time. Outside my tent of evergreens, a few snowflakes drifted down. Falling, blowing leaves made dry, papery sounds. Not far off to my right came a clicking sound, like someone tapping a tree limb. A signal. It unnerved me a little. Probably a buck rubbing the felt off his antlers.

I decided that the five of us treasure hunters should make a pact, a serious one—maybe a blood pact—and think up a code word for the armor pieces, like *the costume,* so people would think we were talking about the play. That'd be perfectly natural, asking each other about *the costume.* And Reece was right, we needed a safer place for the helmet. Strung up in a plastic bag out in the woods—that was no place for a treasure. I could see it swinging in the wind from where I sat. Leaves were falling fast, the woods getting barer by the day. Sure this place was remote, even with the golf cart. But once the leaves fell, the possibility of the sack being discovered or of me being spotted by staff or campers was approaching a hundred percent. I could check on it only after hours, but who wants to be in Telanoo, even on the fringes, in the middle of the night?

We needed a place that was near, but seemed far. Clean and dry. Strangely, Old Pilgrim Church came to mind. But, of course, we couldn't go there. The old man was probably gone, though I'd slacked off watching for him from my window, and couldn't say for sure.

I went back to Great Oak, retrieved the sack, and stashed it in the branches of the thickest cedar. *There. You're safe for now. Even if Reece tells Skid where you are, even if he comes looking, he'll never find you.*

Chapter 10

THE weather turned colder, but "the heat was on," according to Miss Flewharty, our slave-driving director. Miss Flew, as we called her, was very skinny and tall and kind of hunched. She always wore old-fashioned print dresses. Her hair was flat on top and flared out to a dry, frizzy triangle around her chin. She walked loose-kneed with long strides, like she was tired all the time but still had a long way to go. She had us kids do most of the production work ourselves, so we could "learn the ropes," a theatrical term directed mostly at me, I figured. It was my job to keep straight which ropes pull which curtains for which scene changes.

Most after-school rehearsals lasted until . . . "until I say so!" she screeched at the first person to remind her that, according to the printed schedule, we should have been finished an hour ago. She held off mob scenes only by ordering pizzas and chocolate cookies, so we could work straight through. She let a few more cuss words slip every day. According to last year's cast, she'd be cussing like a sailor by opening night, catching herself only when parents were around. Rumor had it she took up smoking too, from the time scripts came in until the stage crew had stored the last prop. The cast and crew worried more about Miss Flew going mental or getting cancer than about getting the lines and cues right.

Somehow, though, we five treasure hunters managed to cram in a powwow during crunch time. It was cold and dark. To keep us from freezing, I built a small fire in the same spot as last time: behind the lake. I brought the makings for campfire pies. Nothing was going on at the camp except a model car club meeting up at the lodge, but the woods seemed a safer place. I'd retrieved the armor pieces from The Cedars before the others came.

I showed everybody how to make the pies using bread and canned pie filling. Reece wasn't hungry. She stared into the fire, her face strangely serious, her hair shiny and gold against her navy sweater. She had on jeans and leather boots and had hardly limped at all down the path to the lake. To say she looked "almost normal" would be shortchanging her. Skid had passed my loyalty test: he'd kept the age of the chain mail a secret from the others. When I broke the news, Robbie whooped, "A thousand years old!? We have ourselves a treasure!" His voice echoed across the lake into Owl Woods. He stared at the helmet resting at Reece's feet in its burlap nest.

"The piece of chain mail is that old," Skid said. "We don't know about the rest."

"A treasure," Reece whispered. "But what kind of treasure?" She locked eyes with Skid across the fire and gave him a drop-dead smile. He winked back. I was so steamed, I almost sacrificed my apple pie to the fires of Camp Mudj.

"Will you guys cut the drama and say what you're thinking?" I demanded.

Reece pulled a Bible out of her knapsack and turned to a place she'd marked.

"This is part of a letter to the ancient people of Ephesus. It was originally written in Greek. It says: 'Therefore put on the full armor of God, so that when the day of evil comes, you may be able to stand your ground, and after you have done everything, to stand. Stand firm then, with the belt of truth buckled around your waist, with the breastplate of righteousness in place, and with your feet fitted with the readiness that comes from the gospel of peace. In addition to all this, take up the shield of faith, with which you can extinguish all the flaming arrows of the evil one.'" She paused, "And here's the part I want you to hear: 'Take the helmet of salvation.'"

She looked up from reading, dead serious. "The armor of God."

I paused for a minute before I laughed out loud. "God's armor? I didn't know he needed armor. I thought he was all-powerful or something."

She gave me that you-poor-idiot look. So I picked up the helmet, stared it in the face, and wise-cracked, "A little outdated, don't you think? Shouldn't this be a bio-mask?" Then I held the helmet up beside my own face, looking out at the others. "Looks like God and I are about the same size."

It was like some creep had taken over my vocal cords.

Mei nibbled at her pie and stared at the fire. Skid shook his head. Even Robbie scowled, and he always laughs at my jokes.

Reece went on as if I hadn't said anything. "God provides armor for his warriors, for protection in battle."

"Battle? What battle?" I asked.

"Spiritual warfare."

"Oh yeah," I pretended to know what she meant. "So how did you know they were Greek letters?"

"Every now and then my Bible study teacher shows pictures of archaeology stuff from Bible times. I remembered that some of the Greek letters looked like English. Also, my mom belonged to a sorority in college, and they use Greek letters."

Skid threw in his two cents worth. "Reece is suggesting that the helmet and arm piece are not just relics."

Robbie seemed to get it. "Otherwise they would be in a big museum, not buried behind a graveyard in Magdeline."

"Exactly," said Skid. "It's more about what they mean."

"Hold it," I said. "That letter in the Bible didn't say anything about an arm piece."

"We're on it," Skid said, pulling a gold-colored high-tech gizmo out of his jacket pocket. It was about an inch thick and small as an index card, but it flipped open to three times that size. He punched in something, and read: "'James, Peter and John, those reputed to be pillars, gave me and Barnabas the right hand of fellowship when they recognized the grace given to me.' That was from the letter to the people of Galatia, second chapter, ninth verse."

He closed the little gizmo. I wondered what it was but didn't want to ask.

He knelt on the ground and spread the arm piece out, very carefully. "See," he said. "It's for the right arm."

"So, what do they mean: the helmet of salvation and the right hand of fellowship?" Robbie asked.

Reece looked down at her Bible. "We don't know . . . yet."

We all got thoughtful. Reece went back to reading the Bible again. Mei pondered, "One thousand years? . . ."

Robbie and I stared into the fire. He asked me quietly, "Do you think it has some kind of power?"

I shrugged. Reece had closed her Bible and was looking up the hill toward Old Pilgrim Church. "Maybe," she answered.

"So what do we do?" I asked, practically.

"We get the rest of it," she said.

I stared at the bronze pieces, engraved with *soterion* and *koinonia*. Firelight danced around on them, making them shimmer and move.

Chapter 11

REECE and Mei were real particular that we not "vandalize" anything, so Robbie carefully pried loose the nails of the boards over the front door and basement window of Old Pilgrim Church, and I did a repeat performance of the first time, crawling into the basement and letting the others in. It was early morning when a heavy fog often lay around the lake. Good cover for us. And this time—once we all got inside—I kept my voice toned down and my ears perked up. We had two flashlights, not one, and a shovel. I had insisted that Skid didn't need to come with us—the fewer, the better. In a surprise move, he agreed; and this time I extended my hand first. When we shook hands, it felt like we were even.

The four of us made a beeline for the furnace and behind it to the plank door, which also had been nailed shut. Someone really didn't want us poking around. No one spoke, but I could see it in their faces. We all were hoping that grave in the crawl space held the rest of the armor, intact after a thousand years and priceless. In the back of my mind, I'd already started a list of things I'd buy with my cut of the money: a new, bigger bow and arrow, some high-powered binoculars, and maybe even my own golf cart, dark green with Indian designs.

Still, when Robbie yanked out the last nail, something came over us. Questions.

What if we were digging into a real grave, which was a crime?

What if the helmet had come from somewhere else?

What if some curse was at work here, and we better not disturb it, or else?

I wondered what Reece and Skid had been whispering about at the campfire. Were we mixed up in something holy?

Not that I was concerned about that kind of stuff, or believed it. Church was for old people, and people who needed stuff, like Reece who needed to think that God could heal her. If I were to choose a belief, it would be the medicine ways of the Creeks. How did a guy get to be a medicine man? What powers could you have? I knew this much: that medicine powers came from vision quests. Someday—maybe next summer—I'd figure a way to get away from home for a few days and go into Telanoo on a vision quest. I'm not ashamed to say the whole idea was pretty scary—no food or water for days, all alone in The Land No One Owns, seeking a guardian spirit. But to learn the medicine ways would be worth it. I would do it . . . someday.

One look in the crawl space yanked me back to the present. The grave was empty!

"It is gone!" whispered Mei. Her voice in the half-dark sounded so disappointed. It was the first time she'd acted like she was really into our quest, that she'd gotten over being scared.

We gathered around the fresh hole. Robbie and Mei pointed their flashlights at it. The hole was about three feet deep, with dirt flung out from it across the small room—a rush job.

Reece, who'd been strangely quiet up to this point, said sadly, "It was all here. The whole armor. And he took it. He tore it apart." She sounded like she was going to cry.

"We'll find it," I said.

"No, we won't! Don't you see? He took it apart and buried pieces of it all over. Or . . ." she gasped in air, panicked. "Or he knows we dug up the helmet and he's destroyed the rest, so we'll never find it!"

"He wouldn't do that," I said. "It's valuable. It may be worth millions. If he does know we have it, if he saw us—" I broke off, but it was too late. Everyone knew what I was thinking.

Robbie gasped at me, "He'll come after us, to get it back!"

We stood there looking at each other, our flashlights casting eerie upward shadows on our faces. I was just beginning to understand what Reece and Skid were hinting at. Maybe the armor had fallen into our hands not by accident, but for some purpose. I didn't have the heart to tell them that the old man probably had seen me the night Robbie and I had watched him bury the helmet and arm piece. If he knew we had part of his precious armor—if he went back and checked that hole beside the reject grave—what would he do to get it all back?

Reece looked up at me, and her sadness really got to me. "What do we do next, Elijah?"

Mei spoke up, and I couldn't believe what she said: "Next step. We find the grandpa."

Reece had Skid absolutely plastered against her locker the next day, practically touching noses with him. I came up quiet, hoping to overhear before they saw me, but all I got was something about "keep it from him."

Keep what? A secret? The helmet?

"Hey, guys," I said with a thin smile.

"Hey, Elijah," Reece greeted me back with a big grin. It looked real, but who can tell with girls? They'll show teeth if they like you, or if they're dragging your name through the mud, or if they want a huge favor.

I wasn't as sure of Reece as I had been a week ago.

"I was asking Skid if he could help us find the old man," she said.

"You said, 'keep it from him.' What did you mean by that?"

She gave me an odd look. "Yeah. We were talking about how we can get him to lead us to the rest of the armor, while keeping it from him that we have two pieces."

Reece saw in my eyes that I was ready to hit the ceiling. "Wait, Elijah," she said, grabbing my arm. "I know what I'm doing. Skid's not part of the inner circle, are you, Skid? He's just helping out. So he can ask around more easily, arouse less suspicion. If any questions are asked, see, he's never been in the church and can say honestly he had nothing to do with the discovery. All he's done is ask a scientist about some old scrap of metal someone found. He can help us lay low."

Miranda Varner walked by and flashed her emerald greens at Skid. She flipped her hair at him and gushed, "Hi, Marcus." His back went all straight, he jerked his head with a, "Hey, Mandy," and watched her until she disappeared in the crowd down the hall.

Boy, I hope he likes her, I thought. *I hope he's crazy over her.*

The bell rang and we scattered like roaches when the lights go on. As Mr. Ridenour went through our assignment, I fumed over why Reece didn't check with me first. After all, it's my camp that borders the graveyard, my tools we've used, my hiding places. So it just follows that any decision about the treasure should be my decision.

Robbie and I got to be in first lunch, thanks to a senior high field trip. I was hoping to have a three-minute powwow with Reece. I got stuck in line while she and Skid snagged a corner table and pored over the Bible, like they had some great secret all to themselves. When Reece would look up to see where I was in line and smile at me, Skid would make goo-goo eyes at Mandy at the next table, then be nose to nose with Reece again.

Boy, talk about having your cake and eating it too. Talk about playing the field! Talk about worming your way into the inner circle—night crawler!

Enough was enough. I had to get control of things.

Okay, I wondered, *say the armor does have power. So do medicine ways. What if I mix them both in a vision quest?* I walked home from school after a stop at the town library to get a book on Indian culture. I made a lame excuse to Robbie that I had to work for Dad and not to call me (which made him suspicious, but too bad). I made an excuse to Mom that I had a project with Robbie and that we'd be at the library (so she wouldn't call Robbie's house), and that I'd stay overnight at The Castle. I packed my gear behind locked doors so the twins wouldn't snoop. Dad's map of the area would help me find a shortcut from Telanoo to school in the morning. I sort of knew the way already: follow Rocky Creek until it branched, follow the east branch up the ridge, then across a couple of hills through the Morgan farm. If I stayed on course, and didn't get charged by one of their Black Angus bulls, I'd come out by Old Railroad Lake across from school.

Geared up—and with a brief stop at The Cedars to get the helmet and arm piece—I hiked deep into Telanoo.

The air was clear and crisp, the trees aflame in late afternoon sun. There was the threat of heavy frost, but I couldn't worry about that. I was on a vision quest, which involved discipline and pain. Besides, this questor knew how to make a fire. I'd thought about taking one of the walkie-talkies, but was pretty sure I'd be out of range. I wanted to leave a note for Mom, just in case, but couldn't risk the twins finding it. I had left a note in my school locker, in case I disappeared.

Telanoo is so different from Camp Mudj, it's like another country. The landscape gets suddenly ragged, where sharp rocks push up through thorny scrub brush. There are no paths and only a few animal tracks. Old creeks have cut deep ravines in the rock. Some have said there are caves. I haven't found any, but some parts of Telanoo I've never explored. Without a compass or the sun or the North Star, you could get lost. Not that you'd wander for miles and die and they'd find your bones years later, not that extreme. But I don't mind saying I kept an eye on the terrain before me, because if I should fall and break a leg, it could be bad. The crunch of my steps and the cold cloud of breath around my face kept me company.

Twilight fell. The trees in Telanoo became sparse and bare, as if I had walked through autumn and into winter in an hour. Then there was nothing but a whole sky of deep red and a straight black horizon, except for one dense grove of tall evergreens to the west, which looked like someone had punched a black hole in the sunset. Like my cedars near Owl Woods, this dense cluster was a good place—shelter from wind and frost, with nice dry tinder for a fire.

I set up camp on a level spot, made a ring of stones, cleared a place for the fire, and gathered wood. When the fire took off, I read the Indian book. Come to find out, I wasn't too young for a vision quest. Crazy Horse was thirteen when he had his, though he hadn't purified himself in the sweat lodge or fasted to connect himself to the sacred powers. But his vision had led him through great battles.

What does it mean to prepare for a vision quest? I wondered.

What magic comes from not eating for three days, and sweating for hours? I felt silly. *How is this supposed to work?* I unwrapped the armor pieces and laid them before the fire. *Soterion*—salvation. *Koinonia*—fellowship.

Indians believe nature and the spirit world work together, the book said. *Are these old pieces of metal connected to another dimension too? Is that what Reece thinks?* I picked up the helmet and looked into its empty face. "Who made you? Who wore you? Did he fight? Did he win, or did he die? Was there more than one who wore you?"

The fire crackled. I was thirsty. I emptied the canteen on the ground instead of drinking it.

I went back over the past weeks, how it all began: from our search for costumes and curtains, to grave-robbing and screaming campers and narrow escapes, to secret meetings about ancient treasure. I poked at the fire. Fire fairies went up into the cedars and disappeared. I was glad it had rained a few days before. Dry boughs above the fire with all these sparks could have put me in a situation.

Maybe the armor is here to teach me something, like how to take control of the group, how to win. I wasn't going to give up the armor until I knew its meaning.

I began to wonder if I should hide it even farther from Great Oak until we decided as a group, as a clan of the same fire, what to do. I just wasn't sure I could trust Skid. With Reece getting friendlier with him, how would I know when she'd be more loyal to his ideas than to mine?

I thought about everything as I looked into the empty face of the armor. I thought of Mom's cooking. It was chicken night; the twins would fight over the wishbone. Dad would probably get a call or two while they ate and have to run and get his clipboard to check on something.

I thought about the shoes I was wearing and which wood makes the best fire. I wondered if I'd forgotten a homework assignment for tomorrow. I thought about what I'd have to kill and eat if I ever had to live out here like a real Indian.

At what exact moment I sensed that I was being watched I don't know. It came in a kind of slow rush, a crawly feeling from head to toe. At first I thought it was the fire dying down, the cold and darkness getting to my back. Then it was in my head, a knowing that I was not alone.

Terror swept through me, then confusion. No one lived in Telanoo, no one crossed it, there were no roads or paths because it led nowhere. *Have I looked too long into the helmet's empty eyes. Am I imagining it's alive? Or is this how visions begin, with sensations of other beings lurking about?* Slowly I looked around. I remembered the skunks and willed myself to be brave in case glowing eyes should come floating in from the darkness. *Has Robbie followed me? Has Skid?*

For a long time nothing happened. *Should I run?* Not a good idea. Even with good night vision, I'd likely break my leg in the dark, trip on a rock, twist my ankle in a crevice, or fall off one of the jagged cliffs. Mom and Dad would never find me. No one would ever come out here.

I stayed put and tried to open my mind to a vision.

Nothing happened, but I was still sure someone was out there.

Courage suddenly seized me. I stood and yelled, "Hey, I know you're there!"

Then . . . above my head . . . a sweep of air—

The flap of giant wings swooped over my head, their span as wide as an eagle's.

My heart died with one *thud,* then started up again, pounding.

A great horned! It was only an owl.

I sat down hard and gulped cold air to calm myself. I read more in the Indian book and studied the helmet.

Though the owl was gone, the feeling of being watched stayed.

And stayed.

But this was a vision quest. Sure, I was scared and I hadn't really prepared for it by fasting and sweating, but I wasn't going to be a coward and leave.

Sometime past midnight, I put the helmet on, then the arm piece. We'd carefully brushed the dirt off, but they still smelled like a hole in the ground. With the ragged leather glove I took up a rock, turning it over, feeling its weight and coldness. *A caveman's weapon.* With my left hand I kept the fire going. And so I sat most of the night.

By dawn, I'd done something I'd live to regret for a year.

Chapter 12

✳✳

"**WHAT** happened to you?!" Reece asked the next morning, passing me in the hall.

I was half-frozen, half-starved, and had terminal bed head. Not to mention I'd run a rugged two miles to school and stood outside sweating and shivering until the school janitor opened the doors. I probably smelled, but with my nose hairs frozen it was hard to tell.

"Nothing," I snapped, and hurried on to class. It wasn't so much how I looked; I just couldn't face her knowing what I'd done. I'd hidden the armor pieces where no one but me could find them. And sitting there in class in a brain fog, I began to wonder if even I'd be able to find them again. I'd stashed them under one of the two million nondescript rocks near one of the half-dozen dry creeks way beyond Owl Woods in the wilds of Telanoo.

I convinced myself this was best, to guarantee that no one was going to do anything with that armor until I approved it. I felt like the armor wanted me to win.

Over the next week, my world unraveled like an old sweater. Reece refused a blood pact because she said it felt like making light of the blood of Jesus—whatever that meant. So I told her—and Robbie later—that the helmet was in my sole possession until we all agreed on the next step.

They all ganged up on me backstage after school. Even Skid was there, and he had nothing to do with the play. Probably Reece had asked him.

"You don't own it!" Robbie snapped. "We all own it!"

"No one *owns* it!" Reece countered, and I was surprised by her anger. "It's . . . it's . . . un-own-able!"

"Owns what?" Miss Flewharty came through the backstage curtains, smelling of smoke. We all froze.

"The costume," Reece blurted out, and bit her lip nervously.

"Yeah," I said, and this is weird, but I really didn't want Reece to have to lie, because I know how she feels about it. So I jumped in. "We were arguing over who gets one of the costumes when the play is over, but I guess it has to stay here in the drama closet."

"Which costume is that?"

"The . . . the coolest costume in . . . the world," I stammered. My mind was a blank. All I could think of were armor pieces glowing in firelight.

Robbie jumped in as if to rescue me, but he was kind of smirking at me when he said, "Elijah wanted to have it for himself. He's kind of—" he made quotes with his fingers "— *in charge* of that costume, so he thinks he has the final say."

Miss Flewharty turned to me, "Injun Joe's costume? It is neat, isn't it, all that leather and beadwork?"

"But nobody's just allowed to *take* costumes, are they, Miss

Flewharty?" Robbie said, snubbing his nose at me.

"Of course not. Costumes are school property. Elijah, if you ever need to borrow something—if your parents are doing a reenactment at the camp, for instance—you might check with me or Mrs. Coyle. We could make arrangements."

"Otherwise it would be—" and Robbie did the quote thing with his fingers again, "*stealing,* wouldn't it, Miss Flewharty, to take something that wasn't yours?"

Right before our eyes, he'd become Sid, the low-down, sniveling brother of Tom Sawyer.

"Oh brother," I said under my breath.

Reece gathered her books like she was leaving. "Well, thanks for clearing that up, Miss Flewharty. I'm really excited about the play. I think it will be great."

"Yes, oh yes," she said, then slid back into director mode. "Now! We have a total of twelve hours—*twelve hours!*—over the next week-and-a-half to whip this show into shape." She turned to Skid. "You'll excuse us." She ousted him off the stage with a nod, told us to find our places, and headed behind the curtain for another smoke.

Robbie and Reece stood there glaring at me. Even Mei, who'd never shown a temper, stood there with her lips tight, her neck stiff, staring hard at the floor.

"We want it back," Robbie hissed. "You get it tonight, or I'm telling!"

"I won't get home until dark!" I hissed right back.

"Use a flashlight," Reece said.

"I don't know if I can find it in the dark!"

Reece put the pieces together quickly and blew a gasket.

"You don't mean . . . you didn't . . . you hid it . . . in *Telanoo!?*"

I didn't answer.

"You hid it way out there in the dark . . ." she said in as unfriendly a tone as I ever heard her use. "That's where you were that night. Why you came to school all messed up. You hid the armor from us, where we could never find it!"

All of a sudden it hit me that it was the most hidden from her. The other kids could go on their own and snoop around for it, but the treasure was absolutely out of her reach.

Her face went all sad and she groaned my name. "Elijah . . . you lied to us."

"I didn't."

Her sadness and anger and disappointment unnerved me more than those invisible eyes watching me from the dark. Her look felt like everything was over.

Chapter 13

FOR the next few days, they wouldn't even look at me. At lunch I sat by Justin Brill, who was playing Injun Joe. I pretended that I had to ask him about his performance, like if the red and blue spotlights on him in the cave scene were good and scary . . . shop talk, so no one would wonder why I wasn't sitting with Robbie.

I guess I'd made my point. Maybe they'd all be a little more careful about who was telling who about our secret, or about who was deciding what about a potentially priceless treasure.

Or maybe I'd just lost all my friends.

Losing friends, it's like . . . well, it's not like anything I can describe. It's not like your heart is broken, because a break you can put a cast on, take a strong pill for, and then go to sleep and feel better. It's more like your heart has the worst case of flu. It aches all over. There's ringing in your ears, the voices of your friends yelling at you. You can't concentrate, your eyes can't see, but your legs still work on automatic pilot and carry you down the hall and in and out of the right classrooms.

I couldn't tell the others my vision quest had fizzled and turned into a helmet-hiding quest. They didn't know anything about vision quests. I was beginning to think that neither did I.

I put a note on their lockers: *My house, then to Tel. for costume. Saturday 2:00.* Anyone else reading those notes in the halls of Magdeline Independent Schools would think the costume people were gathering to make telephone calls. Only the five of us knew what *Tel.* meant.

Saturday afternoon, after I'd done a bunch of work for Dad, Robbie showed up at the lodge, and Mei came too. Skid had left a note on my locker that he'd be out of town.

Reece didn't come. I figured it was because she wouldn't be able to help us search Telanoo.

We got to my vision quest camp easy enough after an hour of hiking. I had intended to draw a map to chart my way out of Telanoo, but it had slipped my mind in the cold and sleeplessness and fear of that night. I'd buried the helmet and arm piece near an *S*-shaped dry creek with a little island of dead grass in it. But in daylight with the sun casting long, cold shadows, everything looked different.

The dry streams each had several *S* curves, and lots of little islands with dead grass. Every flat, fossily rock looked like the one I'd buried the armor pieces under.

We looked all afternoon. I played calm, but panic was creeping in more every minute. We backtracked to the camp and set out again. After another hour of searching, Mei and Robbie were tired and hungry. Me too, but I didn't let on.

Finally—finally!—we found the spot: at a sharp *S* curve in a dry creek—above it on the bank where a flat, fossily rock angled up against another to make a little stash cave. "Here it is! I found it!" I cried. The other two came running, excited. Our hard work had paid off.

I knelt and heaved the rock away, but the armor was gone! I stood there staring at the hole.

"Wrong again!" Robbie whined. "Elijah, why didn't you draw a map or mark it better? What a dumb idea, to hide it under a rock that looks like all the other rocks in—" he spread his hands wide and made a dumb face, "Rock County, U.S.A.!"

"This is the place," I said flatly. "It was here."

They both looked at me, stunned.

"You are sure?" Mei asked, sounding scared.

I looked around, spotted the twin trees landmark I'd missed before—the Nori and Stacy trees I'd named that night and had forgotten about until I saw them again—and the *S* curve in the creek with a tiny, distinct island of tall wild grass. My heart sank.

"I'm sure."

Robbie became Sid again. "Do you think we're stupid? Do you expect us to believe it just walked away?"

"I don't know! I don't know! Maybe Skid followed me," I said, grasping at straws. "I had the feeling that night that I was being watched. Maybe he—"

"Oh, come off it! I can't believe you led us on this wild goose chase."

"I'm telling you the truth!"

"Like you did that night, when you were—" Robbie made

another face, screwing up his features until he looked like a rubber-faced, snarling lunatic, "working for your daaad!"

I came up on my feet and made stiff fists down at my sides. "Hey, you know what, they picked you right for the part of Sid, because you are some big pest! And if you were so suspicious of me that night, maybe you followed me! You wanted it for yourself, so you could dress up like King Arthur!"

"I'm telling your dad! Everything!" he said.

The argument was heading toward a kindergarten fight with us bloodying each other's noses. Then Mei stepped up.

"Who else?" she piped in frantically. "Who would follow?"

"Nobody!" I said, then added desperately, "I don't know . . . Skid, maybe, or Dr. Stallard. The twins follow me sometimes."

I was scraping the bottom of the barrel by suggesting two six-year-olds would stalk me like ninjas through the woods at midnight. Ridiculous. I was hoping Robbie hadn't caught what I said, when he said with a huff, "The twins wouldn't stay out all night in the cold! What a dumb idea. C'mon, Mei. Let's go and leave Mr. Liar and Thief out here to rot!"

"When did you bury it?" Mei asked quietly.

"Just before sunrise. I'd been up all night, feeling someone was watching me. I . . . I didn't mean for this to happen."

I watched them jumping across the brambles from rock to rock, negotiating the tangled underbrush. When they were out of sight, I sat down on a log and stared at the empty hole where I'd last seen our priceless treasure.

Where is it!? I screamed inside. *And what have I done?*

Chapter 14

"FINAL Five" was in full swing, the last five days of touching up the sets and working out lighting cues for *The Adventures of Tom Sawyer.*

The whole school was buzzed about the play. No one was even talking much about sports or anything else. Miss Flewharty was a great director—in spite of her strange ways. She probably could have made it on Broadway, or at least some bigger place, like Columbus. The county newspaper had come to take pictures and put the stars on the first page. It was big stuff for little Magdeline, Ohio, where hot news is the furniture store closing for a week while they bump out a wall to expand.

I was at my post—stage left—during dress rehearsal for Act One when one of the back braces came loose from the un-whitewashed fence. The whole thing toppled backwards against the scrim. The splintery wood caught on the material. For a few seconds the curtain tracks above us swayed and creaked. It looked as if the whole stage was going down. Girls started screaming as the weight of the fence ripped the scrim right down the middle and crashed to the floor. A couple of kids working backstage almost got whacked. Miss Flewharty went into a tirade, and called for a break "NOW!" while we "blankety-blank, half-baked carpenters" repaired it. Three of us stage guys and Injun Joe—who's as tall as me but has fifty pound more muscle—hauled it off in a hurry and started hammering, bickering as to whose fault it was. We decided that Tom Sawyer had pretend-painted on it too hard and pushed it over. We sent a guy up to check the curtain tracks and chains.

The crew set the fence up again and waited, but Miss Flewharty didn't show up. Several minutes passed, and we got a little worried. We all really did like her, even though she could act like a cat thrown in the bathtub when she got mad—all frayed and wild-eyed and snarling.

The assistant director, our student teacher Miss Shiloh, gave us another ten-minute break so she could find Miss Flew. Everyone was wandering off to the drink machines, when Reece strode up to me backstage, and stopped with a little gasp of pain.

"How could you do this!?" she snapped.

She wasn't talking about the un-whitewashed fence falling. Mei must have told her about the search in Telanoo and its lousy end.

"Somebody stole it!" I said. I wondered if I should mention that the old man might have seen me before.

"*You* took it first, without telling us."

I'd never seen her so furious, which threw me off guard, so what I said next came out more accusing than I intended.

"Well, *you guys* were doing things without telling *me!*" I shot back.

"Nothing that would risk the safety of the . . ." Her voice fell to a whisper, she glanced around, *"the costume."*

"You can't know that, Reece. You don't know that Dr. Stallard guy, what he might do if he got his hands on it."

"Oh, for Heaven's sake, Elijah! He can't do *anything* with it now. It's gone!" She winced and closed her eyes and wobbled for a second. I was ready to reach out and steady her, but figured she'd slug me if I tried. "You don't know how important it was to me. You can't know!"

"You think it's magic, or something, with miraculous powers in it. I've heard you talk." I wondered if she believed it could heal her.

"It's not the metal, Elijah, it's the message—the Word— that's powerful."

I kept on defending myself. "But you wouldn't make a pact, so we'd know that everyone would keep their word."

"No, especially not with blood," she preached. "But besides that, the Bible says to let your yes be yes and your no be no."

I threw up my hands. "What does *that* mean?"

"It means to be a person of your word, one who doesn't have to make vows and sign papers in blood. Everyone just naturally trusts a person of integrity."

I whirled to stomp away, but turned back. "You don't trust me now?"

"Deliver the . . . the costume and I might consider it," she shot back sarcastically.

"I'm telling you, someone followed me into Telanoo and took it."

"Who would do that?"

"I don't know . . . Skid . . . or that Dr. Stallard guy. Or the old man."

By this time she was right in my face, her finger nearly pointing up my nose. "You are being paranoid, Elijah Creek. That scientist doesn't know you, or where you live, and doesn't care. The old man never saw us. He may have heard us in the basement, but he didn't see us—" she paused and dropped her finger and huffed.

"We can't know that for sure," I said, wondering if I should tell her what I was afraid of: that he *had* seen me, first when Robbie and I were running from the Virginia creeper fence and again that night I spent alone in Telanoo. Before I could decide, she exploded.

"And Skid?! You're accusing Skid of stalking you into the woods?? He would never, ever steal, especially—" she gritted her teeth and hissed, "the armor." Then so everyone in the commons could hear, she bellowed, *"Skid is honest!!"*

The mention of pure, almighty Skid just set me off. I shot back, "Yeah, well, at least you're in the clear, because *you* couldn't even walk that far!"

Reece reeled back a step, like I'd hit her. The air around us backstage seemed like it was made of glass and I'd just thrown a rock through it. I turned and stormed off so I wouldn't see the look on her face, but just as I turned the corner to the back hallway and almost tripped over a pile of props, I heard her say my name, soft and sad, "Elijah . . ."

The next thing I knew I was outside behind the school.

The ancient treasure pieces—and my hopes of a new golf cart and other cool stuff—didn't mean a thing now. Nothing. Zero. Reece was the real reason I'd wanted that cart, anyway, so she could run without legs, so we could go tearing around the lake and through Owl Woods with the wind blowing in our faces.

Finding treasure was great, but not as great as having my own clan of the same fire, with a huge mystery that was our own and no one else's. What had started as an awesome adventure had collapsed in on itself like a burned-out star.

I threw myself back against the cold brick wall and tried to swallow. The armor was a curse. My vision quest was a bust. I'd lost a priceless treasure.

My friends.

Reece.

Everything.

Who am I now? Just a rotten creep who'd let his smart mouth get way, way out of line. Who is Elijah Creek? A nobody. Less than that. Elijah Creep.

I stood there in the corner where they keep the kitchen garbage cans, breathing the stench of old school lunch garbage, feeling like garbage.

Chapter 15

✳✳

THE rest of rehearsal that night was misery. Miss Flewharty yelled at me for leaving my post. I stayed in the shadows, my face burning, and bolted right after they ran the curtain call. I caught a glimpse of Reece as she limped weakly up to her place center stage, and my first hateful thought was, *she's faking it.* But the real me knew better. More likely, she tried to run to the restroom after I insulted her, to cry in private so no one would ask why, and she pushed herself too hard or tripped along the way.

She had trouble with her lines after the argument too, and Robbie was overacting, playing Sid so snotty that Miss Flewharty cussed at him and told him to tone it down, or the audience would be throwing rotten eggs at him.

Standing alone in the dark backstage watching the play from behind Tom's rickety, un-whitewashed fence, I wondered if the junior high drama department's claim to fame was coming apart at the seams. And if that too was all my fault.

The next morning I faked a stomachache so I could skip school, even though the cast and crew weren't allowed to cut. I swore to myself this would be the last time I'd lie to Mom. But I had to get back to Telanoo for one more search.

Nori and Stacy were off to school. Mom had to go to Chillicothe, and Dad was up to his eyeballs in eighty middle school kids from Hillsboro learning about pioneer days. I left a note in case he should happen to look in on me: *Dad, I'm feeling better so I went to Owl Woods to find something I lost. I'll be back before the girls get home. And if anyone calls, I'll be at the play tonight. No prob. E—*

The sky was a sickly white with no sun to gauge time or direction. Since I never used a compass, relying on my wits instead, I got my bearings by the wind and a general sense of the area. I headed due north before swinging around toward the creek where I'd buried the armor pieces. Once there, I looked in the hole again, as if the helmet might magically reappear and stare up at me. What a welcome, creepy sight that would have been! But there was nothing.

The words kept pushing into my mind, echoing what I'd said to Reece: *you couldn't even walk that far, couldn't even walk . . .*

She loved the armor more than any of us did. Those words carved into it seemed so important to her: *salvation* and *fellowship.* Standing there over that hole with my hands shoved in my pockets to keep them warm, it made perfect sense to me why she'd ask Skid, Mr. World Traveler, to help us with translation. He'd been to Greece, plus he knew Bible stuff.

Much as I tried to justify my actions, everything Reece had done made sense. And everything I had done, didn't. What kind of a person was I, to tear her down and be jealous and mean? How could I ever face her again?

On top of the knoll above the dry creek, I stood on the rock which had once hidden the armor. There wasn't a drop of water in the stream, hardly a shred of life anywhere. The grass had died in the first frost, I guessed. *Frost. Winter coming.* I hadn't noticed how fall was rushing past. Fallen leaves, brown and brittle, rattled across the ground. The last of them were falling now, swirling around my face. Tree limbs above waved in slow motion, dry and black. I felt like I was drying up too, drying and falling. Disappearing into the land. There was no one to help me.

I looked up at the dull sky and whispered for help in an air prayer: *What do I do now?*

I decided right then and there—right out of the blue—to catch the last half day of school. I could snag a ride with one of the maintenance guys making a hardware store run, or walk if I had to. I'd sign myself in and tell Miss Tessa, the school office manager, that Mom would be by later with a note. Which would be true, because I'd leave a note for Mom telling her I felt better and needed to pick up my assignments. All true.

If there was any magic to the armor, it must be black magic. Even though the quest had started out as the coolest thing so far in my life, it had ended up being like the first leg of a roller coaster ride—up, up, up toward wide open sky, then all of a sudden it's good-bye, stomach, and don't forget to write.

So the quest is over. Big deal.

Things would get better again. I just needed to get out

of Telanoo. It was too depressing. From my rocky perch, I surveyed the wasteland one last time and spotted something we'd missed before: a faint trail of flattened grass heading away from Camp Mudj, away from the Morgan farm, toward nowhere. Had Robbie and Mei and me made that path while looking for the hiding place? I didn't think so. Actually, I was sure we hadn't.

But someone had. *Someone has been here and left a trail.*

Mustering all my tracking skills, I followed the disappearing trail over rocks and through scrub bushes. I must have looked like a hound on a rabbit's trail, nosing here and there, back and forth across the terrain. At one point the trail disappeared for almost an hour. I crisscrossed the creek and scoured the landscape for trampled grass or broken twigs, anything, when . . . eureka! A medium smooth-soled mud print on a slab of soapstone in a low swampy spot between two ridges. A footprint. A man's shoe—size nine or ten. Measuring the direction the shoe pointed against the sharp west wind, he had to be heading—as the crow flies—toward the old church.

Who else would follow me into Telanoo and stalk me all night to watch what I'd do with his armor? The old man.

Maybe I should have been worried, but I wasn't. Maybe I shouldn't have felt a burst of hope, but suddenly I did. After all, was it just coincidence that we four kids had checked that crawl space in the first place? Was it just coincidence that Robbie and I had gone spying on the church just in time to see the old man bury the armor pieces behind the cemetery?

We'd found the armor once—twice, actually—and we could do it again.

Providing he didn't melt it down into ashtrays first.

Finders keepers? I thought with resolve. *You may have found it, but we're going to keep it. You buried it, we dug it up; we buried it, you dug it up. It's our turn now.*

I set out in a dead run, nose still on the trail. It was lunchtime. I had to get back home, then to school.

The trail came and went like a ghost. It split off a couple of times into what looked like old trails, not rutted from the weight of heavy, hoofed animals like deer or cows. Maybe I'd been wrong. Maybe people did wander Telanoo in the recent past.

I ended up just where I thought, at the foot of the ridge below Old Pilgrim Church.

My legs carried me in a blur past the graveyard and behind the church. I saw something I'd missed before, and stopped dead. On the side of the church facing away from camp, cut into the wood siding so it hardly could be seen, was a narrow door with no doorknob. It stood a little ajar. I remembered that first night when the four of us came up out of the church basement to find the intruder had vanished. He'd hidden in there. *Could be a tool closet,* I thought, *a good hiding place.* I went up to it cautiously, trying to get a look inside before I got too close. I put my hand on the door and eased it open. Maybe this was where he hid the treasure. Or maybe he was in there. I braced myself and eased it open.

The closet was about two by three feet, and empty except

for a shovel and a scythe, the kind the Grim Reaper carries. In the dirt floor were a few more of those same footprints.

He hides in here.

You'd think I'd be relieved that the toolshed was empty, or disappointed that there was no treasure there. But all of a sudden I was more scared than if a raccoon had jumped out at me, because of what that tool closet told me about the old man.

Old men I know are mostly very nice. My grandpa painted houses and fished a lot before he died. Others I see around town work part-time at the hardware store or sit in Florence's Greasy Cup and drink coffee.

I'd never heard of an old man who hid in abandoned tool closets and followed kids into the woods and spied on them all night in the freezing dark. I never knew an old man who buried things by the light of the moon. We were dealing with a strange, unpredictable person, one who was breathing down the neck of Camp Mudj.

My adrenaline got pumping and I took off, sailing past the back of the lodge where the Hillsboro kids were having lunch. I got to the house, skipped all five steps and flew up to the porch, landing with a *thud*. Once inside, I scribbled off a note to my mom explaining I'd gone to school. I propped it against the saltshaker on the table.

I tore off another piece of paper and wrote a note to stick on Skid's locker. It said, *Skid, I need your help. E—*

Chapter 16

SKID tracked me down after school, acting like everything was fine, and asked what I needed. Maybe Reece hadn't told him what slime I was. Which was hard to believe, that she wouldn't call him up and tell him every single word right away. But as I said before, Reece was different. I explained that I had reason to believe the old man might know something about the armor pieces I'd lost in Telanoo. And since Skid had no part in the play, he'd be free to try and locate him. My description of the old man was pretty sketchy: medium height, thin and hunched, sort of frail-looking. Small head, thin hair.

Skid looked at the note, looked at me and said, "I'm on it." He saluted me with his index finger and sauntered off.

I didn't say anything about the trail I'd found, or the shoe print. Just that finding the old man was our last hope.

The four of us weren't speaking, which was a good thing, since Miss Flew demanded absolute silence backstage during the performances. I don't mind saying that we wowed Magdeline and a herd of incoming relatives on opening night with our acting, costumes, lighting, and sets. They responded with flowers and hugs for the girl actors, whoops for the boy actors, and a standing ovation for the rest of us.

Amazingly, between Friday's and Saturday's shows, Skid got the low-down on the old man, quick as greased lightning. He taped a sealed envelope with my name on it to the backstage fuse box on Saturday night. The note said: *Stanford (Stan) Dowland, age 78, 26 Jewett Drive, Newpoint. Retired, widower, does part-time bookkeeping.* Skid didn't say how he knew this was the guy, only: *He's your man.*

I wanted to tell Robbie I had a lead on the armor thief and ask him to go to Newpoint with me to check it out. A bike trip might help patch things up with him. But since I'd messed things up, and by rights should be the one to fix them, and since I didn't want to be accused of another wild goose chase, I set out alone that cold Sunday morning on the four miles of back road to 26 Jewett Drive.

Stashing my bike in some bushes down the street, I strolled past the house half a dozen times. It was a plain white ranch house at the corner of Jewett and a narrow side street called Crayford, which went up a shrub-lined hill to the left of the house. The blinds were closed. I didn't see lights in any windows.

The attached garage was on the right with the door on the side, and an *L*-shaped driveway leading into it. No sign of a basement, no ground-level windows. The most likely place for pieces of ancient treasure in burlap sacks, then, might be the garage.

What should I do? I wondered. *Stroll up to the front door and announce my presence? Peek in a window? Was it breaking and entering if I didn't break anything, and if I sort of entered by easing the garage door up about eight inches and squeezing under?*

Traffic was sparse in Newpoint early on a Sunday morning. I crossed the street, walked up the driveway, and angled across the backyard like I was heading onto Crayford Avenue. Crossing yards isn't frowned on in my area. Kids do it all the time in Magdeline, coming and going from each others' houses after school.

Three-fourths of the way up the slant of Mr. Dowland's long, narrow yard, I glanced back. I couldn't believe my luck. There was a back door on the garage, and it was standing wide open. I stopped at the edge of his yard under a black locust tree and looked around. *Where is he?* I watched and waited a while. *Why's the door open?*

I ruled out yard work. *Is he out walking a dog? Had the door just blown open? Maybe he's at a neighbor's, having coffee. The longer you wait, Creek, the worse your chances.*

I made a big deal of scratching my head and looking confused, as if I were lost, in case a mom in the neighborhood was washing breakfast dishes at the kitchen sink and spotted me out her window. I cut back across the yard again, curving my path toward the garage. Then I peeked in.

Almost as I'd pictured it, there was a pile of burlap sacks in the corner with a shovel. A dusty blue car hogged most of the space in the garage. I slipped just inside the doorway and pressed myself against the bare stud wall, my heart jack-hammering my ribs.

The car's here. He must be home. Probably asleep. The door must have blown open.

I argued with myself about what to do next. Oddly, I thought about what Reece would do. *Well, she wouldn't go rummaging around in someone's garage without asking, that was for sure. This was a hard call. Mr. Stan Dowland had stolen back the armor, which I had first taken from him and buried in a place that no one owned. And though we had taken it from him first, we hadn't stolen it actually, but found it, and not in a legal church graveyard, but just outside the graveyard, in the dirt next to a reject grave with a blank headstone. So who had rights to it?*

I needed a lawyer.

I was all tied in knots about what to do next when I heard the most horrible, bloodcurdling barking imaginable coming from the yawning doorway. My eyes shot around the corner and landed on a huge, woolly, black malamute tearing across the backyard, his fangs bared, eyes blazing, coming right at me at ferocious speed. At the very instant he bounded through the door, I was up on the roof of the car, half standing, not breathing.

His wild barks cut through the stale air of the little garage. His toenails clawed at the bumper, his weight rocked the car. He wanted at me. If he hadn't been so bulky, and the car hadn't been so slick, he'd have made it up on the hood the first try. I would have been dog food.

I was actually relieved when the old man rushed in and started yelling. I must have looked terrified. He commanded, "Salem! Get down!" When it refused to obey, he grabbed the beast by the collar. Then he started yelling at me.

"What do you think you're doing!?"

"I . . . I . . . came for the helmet . . . sir." It's what Reece would have said: the blunt, unvarnished truth—but with respect.

His thin face went from alarm to pale confusion to flat recognition. He knew who I was: a church-vandal-turned-scared-Indian-boy in the woods, now a burglar surfing on his car roof, trapped. The way he recognized me told me for absolute sure that he'd been the one watching me.

"You! Get out!" he ordered.

"You threw it away . . . sir. Why can't I have it?"

He seethed. "Thrown away and buried are two different things!"

He had a point, but I was stuck on the car for the time being, so I might as well keep pressing. "It's for my friend. She can't walk. She thinks it has power."

"Oh, the armor has power, all right. But not the kind you could handle. No good will come of it." He kind of laughed, but it was a downright unpleasant laugh.

"Then why can't we have it?"

The malamute was yanking at his arm, teeth still bared at me, snarling and drooling. Mr. Dowland took a minute to hoist the dog up the two steps into his house and shut the door. He turned back to me.

"Let it go. You don't know what you're dealing with."

Why I got so bold, I'll never know. He could have let his black beast loose on me with one turn of a doorknob. But I pressed on, "I didn't break in here. The door was open. I'm sorry. And . . . but, I can't let it go, sir, not without knowing the story. For the sake of my friend." Cautiously I slithered off the top of the car to the trunk, my knees still rubbery. I glanced at the sacks in the corner. They looked empty. My feet slid to the floor.

"Give it up," he said, "and get out."

"I'll get out," I said, easing toward the door. The malamute was still barking. I could hear snarling, his claws scraping the paint off the door, his body pressing against the wood, trying its strength. I was pretty terrified, but I thought of Reece and the others, and was just frustrated enough not to care what happened to me. "I'll get out . . . but I can't give that armor up."

"You won't find it."

"I found *you,* didn't I?"

Quickly I calculated the distance between him and the door to his house, and the distance between me and my bike down the street. Gauging my speed against his and his dog's, I could probably just get to it and be off before that fanged creature called Salem could tear me to shreds. I kept one eye on Mr. Dowland's hand.

"I have nothing to say, boy."

But I had something to say to *him,* which just might set him off.

He was facing me, the light from the back door falling on his face. I seriously looked at him for the first time. His eyes were pale blue, but not like Reece's clear sky blues. His were cloudy and not quite focused. His face was very thin and dry, scruffy because he hadn't shaved yet, and carved with deep lines. It struck me that, if Telanoo could be human, its face would look just like his. He hardly had lips, just a thin slit of a mouth, turned down into a frown. He had on a threadbare, green and gray flannel shirt, gray work pants, and beat-up tan tennis shoes. His hair was thin, gray, and greasy, his chin rough and dimply.

Sure enough, Stan Dowland was Telanoo in the flesh.

It was made clear to me looking into that face: he was hiding more than the armor—a secret, deep and dark.

Dark secrets come to the light if you talk to enough people. Someone else besides him had to know the story. I gulped and extended my hand, like Skid had done to me. The right hand of fellowship. Maybe the *upper* hand, if I played my cards right. I flexed the rubber out of my legs.

"My name's Elijah Creek. My dad runs Camp Mudjokivi. And, I'm sorry, sir, but that helmet and arm piece are very, very important to my friend. So, with all due respect, sir . . . if I have to—and what I mean is, if you can't give me a very, very good reason not to—I'll have to start door-to-door, first with 24 Jewett, then 22 Jewett, and so on down the street, asking questions until I know something about why that armor was buried in Old Pilgrim Church." I gulped and took a step back toward the open door. "I'm not giving up, Mr. Dowland. I'm not."

A gray cloud washed over him. His dull eyes settled on me. "It's not worth anything."

"That's okay. All the better."

Right at that moment, nothing mattered to me but having the scary, shining, empty-faced helmet in my hands . . . and someday soon, looking across my campfire to see the faces of Reece and Robbie and Mei smiling back at me.

Even Skid's face would be welcome.

GLOOMY and put out, Mr. Dowland saw that the only way to get me out of his hair was to tell the story. The last thing he wanted was a door-to-door survey of all his neighbors in Newpoint. It was brilliant, I'll admit. But it wasn't really my idea. It just dropped right into my head out of nowhere.

We stood out in his backyard while he told his story of all that went wrong at Old Pilgrim Church, starting fifty years back. I was freezing, but I didn't let on. It was clear to me that he was hungry for someone to talk to. He rambled a lot, and in places the story was boring. On other parts of the story he'd pause to stare off in the distance. When he'd come back from wherever he'd been, his eyes would be half out of focus, looking at me and through me at the same time.

All the while, his black beast of a dog whimpered and groaned at the door, still wanting at me. Mr. Dowland wasn't fazed by the cold. I looked over his shoulder and into the garage at the burlap sacks piled in the corner with the shovel . . . as if . . . as if he hadn't buried the other pieces yet. *Could they be in his house? Maybe the whole thing is propped up in the corner of his living room. Somehow I had to soften him up.*

"Sir," I said when Mr. Dowland took a long break from telling the story. "We were only looking for old costumes or curtains for the school play. We didn't mean any harm."

He nodded, but said with determination, "That armor will be buried where it should have been all along."

"But you dug it up and moved it."

He looked across his yard and across time. His face clouded over, his chin going all stiff. "Yes, I did."

There was another long pause.

"Whatever happened at that church must have been awful," I said with sympathy and even half meant it.

"Rest in peace . . ." he whispered. "With pieces of the past . . . all the dear ones . . . and the others . . . tragedies and truth, a piece with a piece, buried . . . yes, now they will all rest . . . piece by piece they will rest in peace."

Chills on top of chills went down my already frozen back. He went on telling his story as if talking to someone else.

"See, it wasn't right before, but I have it right now. Piece by piece . . . they will rest in peace. Like the ones in the ground," he muttered and then just sort of drifted back into his garage and shut the door.

I retrieved my bike out of the bushes and pedaled full throttle all the way home, even down the hills. It was wide open road. As I struggled in my mind to figure out what to do next, I remembered Mei's words: proceed with caution.

As soon as I got home I wrote out his story as best I could. I still didn't have any hint where the treasure was, but two things were clear: Mr. Stanford Dowland was stranger than a two-story outhouse; and getting the gang together—what I'd hoped for before my trip to Newpoint—had lost all its appeal.

Chapter 17

"Now! All quiet on the set!" barked Miss Flewharty.

It was the last performance and we cast and crew members were getting a little loopy. Robbie outdid himself as Sid. The makeup crew plastered his hair down except for a cowlick on top, which stood straight up. He had extra rouge on his cheeks. With the ridiculous knickers and blousy top, he was a crack-up. He sneered and scrunched his nose right on cue. When Tom—played by Greg Moline—teased him to distraction, he burst into girlish wails and the audience fell on the floor laughing.

Reece had everyone on the edge of their seats. Pale and smiling through pain, she played Becky Thatcher mostly sitting down or standing in one spot, leaning on something. In the scene where she had to walk across the stage, they'd rigged up a walker to look like she was pushing a baby doll carriage. She stayed in character—sweet and fragile Becky Thatcher to a tee. I kept beating myself up over her relapse. It was my stupid insult that did it; either that, or by digging up the armor I'd reactivated a curse.

The lights went down to set up for the next scene. I wheeled the props off stage left, and then came Skid out of nowhere to help Reece stage right. I didn't know it was possible for someone as cool as Skid to ooze all over a girl, but that's just what he did. He sauntered onto that darkened stage, dressed all in black and carrying a cane. He oozed all over her like a big blob of tar, and she melted right back at him. They whispered and held onto each other while she limped

125

off behind the curtain. I stood there watching across the stage with an armload of chairs for the next scene. *Did he sneak backstage under the eagle eye of Miss Flew? Did he join the stage crew at the last minute to be close to Reece?*

All I could do was hope Miranda Varner was in the audience and would miraculously see them in the dark.

I tried to reassure myself that a smooth operator like Skid wouldn't want a girl who may never walk right, no matter how sweet and smart and pretty she was. But a taunt echoed in my head, *Wouldn't be the first time you've been wrong in the past few weeks, Creek. Wouldn't be the first time. . . .*

I had every reason to be depressed. No friends, no armor, no help from old Mr. Dowland. I was itching to watch his house night and day to see where he went and what he did, but I'd have to skip school and camp out in a stranger's yard, not to mention the problem of Salem. Pretty impossible. On top of all that, wintry weather was setting in. This time of year, when the lake freezes and the snow starts falling, I'm always glad we live differently than the Indians in the old days. I'm just spoiled enough to want a roof and a bed, a fireplace, and mom's homemade dinners. Despite the weather, Mr. Dowland's story about the whole armor gave me the courage to try again at what I'd failed at before: a vision quest.

Mei had the sketches of the armor pieces, but she wasn't speaking to me. So I drew my own from memory. They weren't as good as hers, but they'd have to do. I packed them along with another Indian book from the library and my camping gear. I didn't fast and sweat like the Indians usually do before a vision quest, but I did take a long, hot shower with lots of soap, and put on clean clothes. I packed nothing to eat or drink. I told Mom I'd be at Robbie's—so I lied again. But this really was the last time, and before I left, I ran by Dad's office and told him the truth, or sort of—that I'd planned to go to Robbie's (not true) but changed my mind and needed to "go into my cave" (true). It's what Dad says when he needs to be alone. I told him I was going to Owl Woods (also true). But I didn't mention that I was going beyond there into Telanoo.

He gave me a curious look, asked me if there was anything I wanted to talk about. He wasn't prying, because when Dad "goes into his cave" he doesn't want the third degree, so he didn't push it with me either. I'd keep a fire going, I said, and I'd be careful. He told me to take the heavy-duty sleeping bag and the walkie-talkie, which I did, even though the reception breaks up just as you get into Telanoo.

By nightfall my camp was set up beneath Great Oak, due east of its big trunk to fend off a snowy west wind. My tent and sleeping bag would do the rest in the way of protection from the elements. "Shelter is always the first priority," Dad tells the campers in his survival lessons. "Shelter may be a tent, a wool poncho, even forest debris. You can survive several days without food and water. But when it's cold, a person can die in one night without shelter."

I'd picked up a lot of wilderness skills living at Camp

Mudj: how to soak up dew in a bandanna and wring it into a cup, how to spot edible plants, how to make a splint. I'd been working on traveling barefoot, so I took off my shoes and socks while I gathered wood and leaves to build a small fire. The ground was like ice. But vision quests aren't about being comfortable.

Ready to begin, I put the Indian book on one knee and read a couple of paragraphs about how the Indians used an eagle-bone whistle in their powwows to call the Great Spirit. Then I looked at the sketches of the helmet and arm piece. If there were a connection between the armor pieces and the spirit world, this was the only way I knew to find it.

I'd forgotten most of the Bible verses Reece had read, but one phrase kept coming to me like an echo in my head, not in her voice, another voice: *Put on the full armor of God. Put on the full armor of God.*

How am I supposed to put it on if I don't have it? Thoughts danced around. The campfire flamed and flickered in the night wind. But nothing special came. Reading the Bible seemed to give Reece and Skid a kind of confidence. But I just didn't get it. Sure, there were cool stories like global floods and man-eating fish and even a witch and visions of seven-headed dragons and all that, according to Reece. But so what?

I'd forgotten what happens when somebody puts on the armor. Reece had explained it, but sometimes when she goes long talking about church things, I drift off.

The wind picked up, whispering through The Cedars just north of my campsite. The "tall brothers" as the Creek Indians call them, thick and black against the dark blue sky, breathed cold messages to me. I slowly rose to my feet. I listened, but couldn't understand anything. That phrase came again inside my head. *Put on the full armor of God.*

I kept watching that dark grove of evergreens, half expecting a great horned to come swooping out, or the shiny-eyed skunks, or even Mr. Dowland to come forth. I braced myself for a scene like the one from the old movie *The Screaming Skull,* where this big skull the size of a hot air balloon comes floating out of the dark.

Someone was in those trees, sure as I was standing there barefoot and alone. Slowly I tucked the sketches in the book and laid it down on the ground. I put more wood on the fire. I walked barefoot away from the camp directly toward The Cedars.

I know you're in there, I thought.

The fire to my back cast my phantom shadow ahead.

I know you're in there.

Strangely calm, I parted the branches and weaved through the trees until I was in the center of darkness. I couldn't see my hand before my face. I couldn't speak. If it was Dowland, I would have heard his feet, even on the soft, dead needles, even over the moan of the night wind.

Someone had been there. I felt him. I turned and looked back at my campsite, to see what he'd seen as he watched me:

a little fire, no more than a mesh of glowing light through the thick cedar branches; a little tent, nestled up against the gigantic trunk of Great Oak; and me sitting there reading. That's how he'd seen me.

Great Spirit, I thought suddenly. *Master of Breath.*

Was it him, was it really him, and was he trying to tell me something?

All of my senses concentrated. Every cell felt alive. Suddenly I could see that I was small and alone. My tall brothers, the trees, were bigger and older and stronger, but they were alive to help me. My fire burned a tiny spot in a dark, cold night, but it was enough for me. I was going to be okay.

And I knew—with no one saying the words—that even when I'm alone, I'm not alone.

The wind suddenly died and there was no sound, none at all. I knew someone was there. A calm like nothing I'd ever felt came over me. I'm not a crier, but I don't mind saying my throat tightened and my eyes watered.

No glowing eyes came, no screaming skull—just the quietest quiet in the universe.

It was like the Master of Breath was holding his breath for my benefit, so I could hear things . . . like my own heart, and the ocean roaring a thousand miles away.

I heard the trees settling in for the winter.

I heard starlight fall.

Time passed.

At long last, I got the nerve to speak.

"How can I put on the armor, if I don't have it?" I asked, terrified of hearing a voice from the night.

Nothing came, so I asked again.

Still nothing, so once more I asked.

To my mind came the picture of that forked path through Telanoo. I had taken the path up the hill to Old Pilgrim Church. But the other path—grassy and trampled—where did it lead?

A voice inside my head, which sounded like myself only more confident, said: *Get it.*

Chapter 18

IT was the hardest thing I'd ever done, calling a meeting of everyone—Robbie and Reece and Mei and Skid—to spill my guts all over the place and apologize. But I knew that I had to do it. Yeah, it was hard, but in another way it was easy, like bush hogging with Dad when we pull out stumps and thorns to make new paths through the camp. Or like when he and I built the road to the maintenance garage last year, just him and me, arranging bedrock, raking gravel all day long in July heat. It was hard work but good work. Every day I see that road and know what I can do with Dad and me working together. I looked at this meeting like building a new road.

What had really happened to me at Great Oak? I didn't see anything or hear anything other than my own thoughts and that one verse from the Bible. But whatever it was had changed me. Not a whole lot, but enough for me to notice. And enough for me to realize that I needed to come clean.

Before school I wrote out the invitations to the meeting with a big *Please!* at the end. I tucked a wild bird feather and an Indian bead on a leather string in each envelope: red for Robbie, yellow for Mei, black for Skid, and white for Reece. I wasn't trying to bribe them to come; it was more like a peace offering.

I planned to apologize to Reece first, since that was most important. I was afraid she wouldn't come—and with good reason. Really, honestly, I had no excuse for saying that horrible thing to her; it was just me being a punk.

I built a fire in the lodge and began to gather a tray full of stuff—another benefit of living at Camp Mudj. There were stashes of drinks and snacks all over—at the house, in the lodge and cafeteria. I grabbed cocoa and cider packets, trail mix and granola bars, and little pop-open cans of fruit, and beans and franks. I had a banquet ready.

The fire burned strong, casting gold flickers on the vaulted, knotty pine ceiling. No need for lights.

Robbie came in first. "Hey," was all he said. I asked him to help me scoot the couch and recliners close around the fireplace. He got the water going for the drink mixes. Skid came in next, sauntered to the couch without a word, plopped down, and stretched his feet out toward the hearth.

"Hey," I said. "Thanks for coming."

He eyed me coolly.

When Mei came in alone, my stomach sank. She was always Reece's shadow, and you can't have a shadow without the real thing, but there she was. She sat down and folded her hands in her lap and looked at them. I wanted to ask if anyone had seen Reece, but the words wouldn't come.

"Help yourself," I said, spreading my hand to the food lined up on the hearth, as if I was the headwaiter at a fancy restaurant and here was my elegant spread. Skid must have made that same comparison, because one corner of his mouth curled in what could only be called a smirk.

This was going to be hard, and Skid's superior attitude—arms folded, staring at the fire, not getting so much as a drink—made it harder. Whether he'd heard what I said to Reece, or whether he just hated my guts for being myself, was hard to say.

There was nothing but three lonely sounds in the lodge: Robbie tearing open a drink packet, the pouring of water, and the crackling of the fire. I sat cross-legged on the floor and cleared my throat. "If everyone has what they want to eat, I want to begin by apologizing. Um . . . I was . . . kind of hoping that . . . uh . . . that we could all be here for this."

Dead silence followed. If they knew where Reece was, no one was willing to say. I'd stepped in quicksand and nobody had so much as a twig to reach to me. Not even Robbie.

Then the door opened.

My heart went *thump.*

A gust of cold air rushed across the floor, and Reece came around the corner of the entryway and stopped, holding onto the wall for support. Across the room in shadowy firelight with her blond hair, white sweater and corduroys, she could have been a ghost or an angel. Robbie and Mei turned. Skid kept his eyes on the fire with that half-smile on his face. The door slammed shut. She started across the room haltingly. I stood to go help her, but her hand went up and fire flashed in her eyes, her jaw clenched in determination. Every step hurt her, but she kept coming without her cane. She was saying to me, *I can walk, you idiot, you despicable creep. See, I can get that far.* She stomped on me with every step and I deserved it.

I turned to the fire and made a big project of fixing her a cup of hot cider, her favorite, until she got seated. I presented it. She looked blandly into the cup. "I'd prefer something else."

"Hot chocolate?"

She nodded.

"Sure, no prob," I said.

Mei asked Reece how she was. She said fine.

Skid smiled at her and said, *"Maranatha,"* and she grinned back.

So now they have secret code words? It doesn't matter. I'll say my piece and be done, apologize to Reece for saying the cruelest words in the world, apologize to the group for losing our priceless treasure, then they'll go home and I'll go run blindfolded and barefoot through Telanoo and off some cliff.

(Not really, but that's how I felt at the time.)

I gave her the mug of cocoa and bag of marshmallows—so she could get as many she wanted—then I sat cross-legged by the fire again. They say if you encounter a pack of hungry wolves, drop your eyes and get in a lower position to show you don't want to fight.

"The first thing I have to say is to Reece," I began. My throat clogged. I swallowed, coughed, took a breath. "I'm sorry. I don't know what happened to me. I was crazy and mean to talk to you that way."

I would have gone on and told her the big reason I wanted to sell the helmet was so I could have my own golf cart and take her for rides, because I wished for her more than walking; I wished she could fly—

"It's all right, Elijah," Reece said.

"No," I objected. "It's not all right."

"Okay. I just mean you're forgiven."

"Oh." I sat there like a knot on a log. What in the world do you say when someone forgives you? What does it mean? Darned if I knew. Do you say thanks or cool or wow or *sugoi?*

I looked up at her. She smiled and shrugged like it was no big deal. She took a sip of her hot chocolate. Just like that I'd come up out of the quicksand and stood clean on solid ground. Just like that. I couldn't believe I was so off the hook. "Great . . . thanks. I'm really sorry."

Skid chuckled low, which just fried me.

"And?" she asked.

"And I'm sorry about trying to push the blood oath."

"No, I mean what else are we here to discuss? You don't have to keep apologizing, Elijah."

"I know, but in your religion blood's holy or something, and I knew that."

"I don't believe it's holy, just that 'the blood is the life,'" she said simply. I knew it was from the Bible because when she quotes verses, her voice changes; it gets quiet, but strong.

Everyone was looking at me. "And I'm sorry to you all

about the armor. Since it was me who got us into the church, since it all happened on my turf, I thought I had more claim than the rest of you. And I was suspicious of bringing Skid into the group." I glanced at him. "I'm sorry about that too."

Skid's eyes drifted to the fire, and for a minute I thought that was it. He'd written me off. Then his eyes slid back to me. "You can trust me, Elijah Creek. Skidmore men keep their word. We didn't used to . . . but we do now."

"Thanks."

Having felt lower than a snail trail a few minutes ago, I could hardly believe how clearing the air could lift a man's spirits. All of a sudden I was happy, and starved. I reached for a can of beans and franks, popped it open, and started stabbing in it with a plastic fork.

"Elijah?" Mei asked. "The armor? It is really lost?"

How could I forget the other half of my agenda? "Oh, yeah. Good news, bad news. It's a long story so get comfortable," I answered.

Chapter 19

THE wind picked up and whistled down the chimney flue. Skid finally got something to eat, and even said the banquet was a good idea. We all gathered in around the fireplace—me on the floor with my back to the heat and everyone else scooted up close, faces aglow. The rest of the lodge was dark except for red exit signs over the doors. The smell of wood smoke mingled with hot spiced cider.

Reece grilled me on details about the church as I laid out Mr. Dowland's story about how he'd come to Magdeline fifty years ago to a church that was already a century old.

"Dowland said they were a close-knit bunch, mostly friends and relatives, and always had a big choir for the cantatas at Christmas and Easter. Old Pilgrim was known for its fellowship dinners, I guess, because the old guy smiled and looked proud when he said, 'Oh, the feasts those women could spread in that basement! People had to eat standing up sometimes on those occasions!'"

Robbie shivered. "Big dinners? In that creepy, rat-infested old hole?"

"I'm sure it was nicer then," defended Reece. "Go on, Elijah, and don't leave anything out."

"Still the church didn't grow. They only added numbers when babies were born, and lost when people moved away or died. The minister wasn't happy with the slow growth, but the church people were content with themselves. One summer, the minister took his family to Europe to trace the family roots. When they got to Ireland, he bought a suit of armor from a gift shop in an old castle. The armor wasn't a real relic, you see, because an appraiser in the village had said it was pieced and patched, and had the marks of unknown armorers, meaning that each piece was made at a different time and place. There wasn't any record of the armor being used in a battle, even though it showed some wear. It wasn't fancy enough for royal processions, and the words engraved on it devalued the whole thing even more. The armor was just an oddity, the appraiser had said, a big trinket and not worth much."

"Not worth much!?" Robbie asked, as if I'd offended him. "Didn't they know a piece of it is a thousand years old?"

"You mean the chain mail?" I shrugged. "How should I know? But here's where I caught a clue, guys. When Mr. Dowland was talking about the minister's ancestral home in Ireland, once or twice he almost said 'my' instead of 'his.' I think the preacher was Stan Dowland himself, though he tried to make him sound like someone else."

"Reaallly?" Reece was hanging on my every word.

"When I told him I knew what the Greek words meant, he stared at me so hard I got really spooked. Anyway, as the story went, the minister started preaching sermons on the armor of God, to get the people fired up. That's when strange things began to occur."

"What strange things?" Robbie asked.

"I'll get to that. He said the trouble started in the thirteenth year and—"

"Thirteen's bad luck!" Robbie broke in.

"No such thing," Reece snapped. "What began to happen, Elijah?"

At that moment a door opened and a big whoosh of air rushed across the floor. The fire sputtered and almost went out. Mei gasped.

"It's just Bo, doing security," I reassured her, and went on after I'd poked the fire back to life. "The minister thought some strong sermons about being in the service of the king would wake people up. So he propped the armor up beside the Christian flag and they all sang 'Onward Christian Soldiers.' After that I kind of lost track. But for the important details, here's the rest, close to the way he told it: The congregation slowly disintegrated. Tragedies and mishaps came in a steady stream. One of the factories in town closed down, then another. Some people moved away, some died, some drifted. The nursery had a dry spell when there were no babies. Dowland's face went gray when he said, 'Just when we thought the misfortunes were over, another terrible thing swept through the church, a thing that can't be explained by common sense, a thing no family should ever have to go through.' He focused in on me at that point, and practically snarled."

"What was the terrible thing?" Mei asked.

"He wouldn't say, but he blamed the armor. I asked him if he thought it was a curse."

When no one laughed at me, I went on, cautious of sounding too weird. "To be honest, that very thing had been in the back of my mind."

They seemed to be taking me seriously. I looked at Reece. "Especially since you and Skid mentioned something about demon powers. Or I wondered if maybe the church was built on sacred Indian burial ground." I laughed. "My own life has been pretty wrecked since that first twilight when we broke into the church. Dowland himself said, 'See for yourself, boy. The church closed down, locked its doors forever.'"

"The minister buried the armor of God?" Reece said seriously.

"I asked Dowland how he knew where it was. He claimed the minister was his friend and had told him, but nobody else."

"Very convenient," Robbie said in a Sherlock Holmes voice.

"When I asked Dowland where the minister was, he said in a low, quivery voice, 'He's dead.' Chills went through me."

Reece's eyes were wide. "You think he's talking about himself?"

"He is," Skid murmured.

We all looked at Skid, who peered at us like a sleepy cat with his eyes half closed. "I did a little more digging in *The Magdeline Messenger* archives," he said. "It's just as you said, Creek."

Turns out Skid had been busy with a little sleuthing. *He is sort of useful after all,* I told myself.

Skid went around behind me and put another log on the fire before flopping back on the couch. I could tell Robbie wanted to yell at him for keeping that juicy piece of information to himself the whole time, but didn't have the nerve.

I went on with the story. "Then Dowland and I got into a big argument. I said to him, 'So, if the armor was left by the minister and he's dead and I found it, that means you stole it from me!'"

"You didn't!" Reece said, shocked but grinning. Mei and Robbie were hanging on my every word. Even Skid's eyes were fixed solidly on me. Spurred on by their excitement, I reenacted the next conversation, mocking Dowland's gravelly voice, then using my own—pitched higher for contrast:

"'I didn't steal the armor from you, boy. It's not yours!'"

"'But Mr. Dowland, sir, it's not yours, either; it's the minister's, and he's dead!'"

"'That's right, boy! He's dead!'"

"'And why did you wait all night in the freezing cold to get it back from me—a cursed thing everyone was glad to be rid of? It doesn't make sense.'"

Reece's mouth hung open in amazement. "What'd he say to that?"

"Oh, he was madder by the minute, but I didn't back down; I faced right up to him. He just stared off into space and said, 'I did it for the minister.'"

Robbie said in a tone of eerie wonder. "So it was Stan Dowland who bought the armor, cursed the church, and made it close down."

"The church didn't close down," Reece said flatly.

"Hel-l-lo!" Robbie replied in singsong disbelief. "Didn't close?! Where have you been?"

"Pipe down," I told him, detecting a little of Sid still left in him from the play.

"The church never closes down," Reece insisted.

"But the doors and windows are all boarded up," Robbie pressed.

"The church is the people who believe in God. It's not the building where they meet. The church never stops, no matter what. The building over there is ruined and abandoned, but the church goes on."

I thought about it a minute. "The church is . . . people?"

"Yes," said Reece.

"Weird. I always thought it was . . . maybe I didn't think much about it."

Mei had been sitting quietly on the floor, warming her hands around her cup of cider. "How long did all these things happen to Mr. Dowland?"

"He didn't say."

"Fifty minus thirteen?" she figured. "The armor came thirty-seven years ago. It caused the trouble. He buried it. We found it. He moved it, buried it again?"

"Looks that way," I answered. "Or he's in the process."

"Where?" Mei asked.

I shrugged. "There's no way of knowing. At the end of his story, he started drifting off, muttering a riddle about a piece of the past with each piece. Then he said, 'Piece by piece they will rest in peace,' and something about 'pieces of the past.' That was his phrase. I'm telling you he doesn't want the armor found. But for some bizarre reason, he still wants control of it. Why else would he follow me into Telanoo, watch all night in the cold, and follow me the next morning to see where I put it?"

Frightened, Mei asked, "Why would an old man do that, hide and watch?"

"I don't know. But I do know one thing: he's not at all happy about our quest."

"He's daft," said Robbie.

"What is daft?" she asked.

Robbie crossed his eyes and drew circles around his ear. It must be the international symbol for crazy, because Mei understood.

Skid propped up on one elbow. "So, Creek, what's the good news and what's the bad?"

"The good news is that it looks like he's still got the armor. I saw burlap bags in his garage, which may mean it's even in his house. The bad news is that he's not about to let us have it."

"Why did he not throw it away in the garbage, if it is cursed?" Mei asked.

There was a long, thinking pause. Three ideas were put forth, and we ended up thinking all three might be true: that

Mr. Dowland thought the armor had powerful magic, and destroying it would cause him harm; that "pieces of the past" meant that there was something sentimental attached to each piece and he just couldn't bring himself to destroy it; and that despite how strong he talked, he left open the idea of retrieving the armor sometime in the future.

"For what reason?" I wondered out loud.

Skid and Reece eyed each other mysteriously.

"What?" I asked them.

Robbie perked up, "You know, he could be lying about the whole curse, just to keep us away, to scare us."

"But we're not scared," said Reece.

"I believe his story," I said firmly. "He started getting really sad at the end. Old men don't choke up and go cosmic on you if they're making up tales."

Skid said, "If he'd wanted to scare us off his treasure, he would have done a better job of storytelling, making up tales of people strangled in their sleep by the arm, and eyes glowing red from the helmet."

Robbie jumped in, "Yeah! Or whoever possesses it bursts into flame. Good stuff."

I agreed. "A lot of his story was boring. I left out the details about whose mother came down with what ailment after so-and-so was laid up because of which freak accident just before this person and that person went bankrupt. There's no way I could keep it straight, especially with all that snarling and clawing at the door the whole time."

"What snarling and clawing?!" Reece asked.

"His demon dog Salem. It had my hair standing on end," I said with drama. "I came this close to being dog chow. You should have seen the fangs!"

"Demon dog?" Robbie's eyes popped.

They were on the edge of their seats. So I told that part of it. Skid slowly sat up on the couch. Feet on the floor, arms folded and resting on his knees, he studied me. When I finished the dog part of the story, he said, "Whoa . . . you're the man, Creek. You are the man." There was actual admiration in his voice. He reached forward and high-fived me.

Reece shuddered. "You can never, ever go to his house again! Not for the treasure, not for anything!"

"Salem . . ." Robbie said thoughtfully. "That's where those witch trials were, in the 1600s. He named his dog after a witch town!"

The coals had been dying down for a while, but the crackling of the fire had been getting strangely louder. Mei was the first to say something about it. We all perked up and suddenly noticed that, though the fire was low, there was a bright glow on the ceiling. It wasn't coming from the fireplace, but from the high windows at the back of the lodge. A red glow . . .

"What is *that?*" Mei asked fearfully.

We guys were past the kitchen and at the back door in a flash. Skid pushed it open and our mouths dropped.

Robbie screamed, "The church is on fire!!"

Chapter 20

THE fire horns blared. Police sirens wailed. It was the second time that fall Camp Mudj had brought out the local forces.

Fire shot out the church windows and through the roof heavenward. I never knew until that moment the nature of fire when it devours a building. The fire knows it has won when the building starts groaning and falling. The fire gets angrier for a short while, when it realizes there will soon be nothing left for it to consume. Its rage becomes the roars of a dying animal, then everything collapses to smoke and ashes. I came away from that night with a new respect for the power and destruction of fire.

The five of us huddled in the back doorway of the lodge with our coats wrapped around us, watching in disbelief until the old steeple tottered and fell. Its huge, forgotten bell crashed into the flames. One hollow *gong* rang out through the roar and echoed across the camp.

In a pitiful few minutes, the old building was a smoldering wreck.

It was an amazing thing to see. Even sort of cool. But when the firemen came over to the lodge, and I saw the look on Dad's face, reality set in. He was afraid sparks could still make it to the lodge, if the wind should whip south.

Since I was the one to call it in, the police came into the lodge and questioned us. The five of us had the name Dowland in the front of our minds, but a secret understanding passed between us. We couldn't accuse a sad old man, not without proof behind it.

With a lump in my throat, I wondered what they'd find in the ashes.

The fire was big news around town. Nobody knew how it started. I figured it had to be arson, unless those basement rats had taken up smoking. I worried most that it was an omen, or a warning, directed at me.

The mid-term test schedule put the five of us in second lunch. The chicken and noodles were all gone and we were left with—

"What is it?" Robbie asked, lagging at the end of the line.

"It's called corned beef hash," Skid said, curling his lip in disgust. "I brought lunch."

One look at pink meat and white chunks swimming in grease, and Robbie whined, "Corned beef *trash!*"

There were green beans with fake ham cubes—not too bad—and bread and butter. We all passed on the rock hard, slimy pears, except for Mei. We took our trays to the far table and sat. Skid had a couple of steak fajitas.

"Okay, Elijah," Reece said, "tell us again what Mr. Dowland

said about burying the armor—his exact words." She wasn't about to give up.

"He said it would be buried where it should be, where it should have been all along. That was right before he started going weird on me." I pulled my notes from my jeans pocket and unfolded them on the table. "'With pieces of the past . . . all the dear ones . . . and the others . . . tragedies and truth, a piece with a piece, buried . . . yes, now they will all rest.' Then he said, 'See, it wasn't right before, but I have it right now. Piece by piece they will rest in peace. Like the ones in the ground.'"

Reece grabbed the paper and read it to herself, again and again.

With a mouthful of corned beef trash, Robbie asked, "By the way, Skid, how'd you find him?"

"Microfiche and grandpeople."

"What is that?" Mei asked, cutting her pear with a knife and fork.

"Old library files of newspapers, stored on microfilm. And grandparents—they may not be able to remember your name, but they don't miss a lick about every detail from decades back. I went into Florence's on Saturday morning, got a cup of coffee, and sat down with the Romeo Club."

"Romeo?" asked Mei.

"It's code for Really Old Men Eating Out," I said.

None of us could believe that Skid had gone there by himself and sat with a table of old men in broad daylight.

Kids hung out at the Whippy Dip, never ever at Florence's. It was social suicide.

Robbie said to Skid, "You are loons, man!"

Mei said, *"Sugoi!"*

I said, "You're the man, Skidmore."

Even Reece said, "You're kidding!" and looked up from the paper finally. "We need to make copies of this. Study it and see what we come up with. I think it means there are other graves where things are buried."

"Or will be," said Skid cryptically.

"He means each piece in its own grave?" Robbie asked me, as if I should know. "Or is he talking about us?"

Skid shook his head. "'A piece with a piece' means two pieces together. We found two pieces."

"But what does it mean, 'with pieces of the past'?" Reece asked. "Could there be a mystery buried with each piece? A clue, a memento of the terrible thing that happened?"

"If that were true," Skid said, "there would have been a memento with the helmet."

"There was nothing extra in the sack but an old dirty piece of cloth."

Mei had been fishing potato chunks out of the hash on her plate. Thoughtfully, she sucked air between her teeth, which some Japanese people do when they're puzzled.

"The cloth," she said. "It was piece of blanket."

"That was just to keep the chain mail from falling apart," I said.

"Maybe not," said Reece.

This set us off in a new direction. We speculated over the cloth until second lunch was about over, when Robbie piped up, "You know, guys, I wanted this as much as anybody. A piece of armor would be cool to have. But this is a lot of trouble for what the old guy himself called a trinket."

We stopped and thought. Sad to say, Robbie had a point. Our chances of ever finding the whole thing were slim to none. But his words were like a hammer to my chest.

"Give up? That's crazy! *You're* loons!" I blurted out. "Do what you want, but I can't stop. I have to find the whole armor, I have to find it and put it on, like I was told: 'Put on the full armor of God'!"

Everyone gaped at me. I'd said the words like Reece had said them, strong and ringing with authority. Even I was surprised.

Reece shot a glance at Skid.

I got uneasy. "What? What was that look for?"

"Something happened to you, didn't it?" she asked.

Skid had a sneaky half-smile and a downright friendly gleam in his eye.

So I told them as quick as I could about the night at Great Oak, the presence in The Cedars, and the words that came into my mind from nowhere.

Robbie said, "Well, you can't wear what you can't find."

"Yeah, that's what I thought—"

Skid broke in, "If he tells you to wear it, he will help you find it."

Reece broke into a wide grin, ear to ear.

"Who? What?" I asked them. "What are you guys thinking?"

"He spoke to you," Skid said.

"Who?"

"God," said Reece.

I'd thought as much myself, but still couldn't believe it in the light of a new day. I pushed back from the table and shook my head. "Nuh . . . nah, I remembered a verse you read, that's all."

"That's how he does it sometimes," Skid said.

"*Many* times, that's how he does it—through his Word," Reece insisted.

"Why would . . . God talk to me?"

"He wants to use you!" Reece said excitedly.

I didn't like the sound of that. To me *used* meant "used up," like the year before when I sort of liked Pamela Welch—and she found out, and invited me on a picnic with her family, but just to make her boyfriend jealous. When he wanted her back, she dropped me like a hot potato. Nobody likes to be used, but the way Reece sounded, God using you was the coolest thing in the world.

She bubbled over. "It's not lost forever!"

"Hold on!" I objected. "Suddenly I feel like this is all on my shoulders."

"It is, bud," Skid said in friendly fashion. "You got the call."

"How could I get a call from God when I'm not sure I believe in him?"

"He must believe in you."

I looked at Robbie to see if he was getting any of this—him being the brains of the family—but he was busy poking his fork into Mei's cup of petrified pears. *What was I supposed to do?*

Chapter 21

THE cause of the fire was ruled inconclusive, mostly because nobody cared much to do any deep investigating. Dad and the rest of the town were plain glad to be shed of an eyesore and a nuisance. I went over just once when no one was around and looked into the charred hole, feeling the faintest twinge of hope that I'd see something round and metallic. I doubted even the hardest metal could survive that inferno.

The eerie newspaper headline read "Old Pilgrim Burns," and only gave a couple of short paragraphs about when it was built and how many ministers it had. Doing a little math showed me that once the armor came, the church had lasted only seven years.

I couldn't help being morbidly curious about where Dowland was at that moment, if he'd set the fire himself, or if he'd died in it. I wondered who'd feed his dog if he never returned. I, for one, wouldn't be offering to break into that house to check if poor old Salem needed something to gnaw on!

A blue haze drifted up from the ashes, and all of Camp Mudjokivi smelled like smoke for the next few days. Plans were discussed to fill the hole of the ruin before the ground froze.

There was no school the next day because of parent-teacher conferences, and since the gang was all passing, and pretty much behaving ourselves, it was a free day. We decided on another all-nighter—to plan our next move, maybe scout around the camp for more clues—and the parents actually said okay. Bo was pulling more late security duty since the fire, doing stuff in the upstairs lodge office in between rounds; so we'd be semi-chaperoned. Besides that, every living, breathing soul on the planet trusted Reece and Mei. Robbie, Skid, and I were innocent of any possible mischief just by association.

I pulled our five best sleeping bags out of storage, and made the lodge furniture into a tight, cushy semicircle around the fireplace. Mom sprung for pizzas for us.

Everyone had gotten together and decided to wear the beads on leather strings I'd given them, which was very cool. I'd have to make one for myself, a green one. *Maybe,* I thought, *just maybe the five of us could be a clan of the same fire.*

I told them how I'd pictured the forked path in my mind at The Cedars, how curious it all was, a path in Telanoo. No one but me had seen *The Screaming Skull,* so we watched that and had a good laugh. There were some scary parts all right, but the acting was so bad, you could hardly feel sorry about what happened to the victims.

We were all warm and cozy in that otherwise big dark room. As the night wound down, Robbie burrowed into his bag in front of the fire, like a hibernating bunny with just his eyes peeking out. Reece wrapped herself in a recliner, so Mei followed suit in the other recliner. Skid stretched out flat on the couch in between and folded his arms and closed his eyes like he was dead. I was on the floor, propped against Mei's recliner facing Reece, and looking up Skid's nostrils.

Occasionally a door opened and a draft crept across the floor as Bo came in and out on his rounds. The five of us took turns keeping the fire stoked. Even Reece did. It took her longer and she could lift only the small logs, but no one said, "Here, you rest. I'll do that for you." Being included was important to her.

"Nice fire," I said.

"Yeah," she said back.

Mei fell asleep sitting up, and was slumped over, rubber-spined.

"She'll break her neck," I whispered to Reece.

"The Japanese learn to sleep on the buses and trains," Skid muttered. "They can sleep standing up." His eyelids drooped.

The long, thinking pauses got longer and kind of nice as the night wore on to wee hours. Reece wanted to know in detail about my "call." I told her everything, even the creepy-but-cool feeling that I heard the trees settling in for the winter and starlight falling. She thought that was a beautiful thing.

"It's your turn now," I said to Reece. "Explain again about the power."

Reece reached her hand out of her sleeping bag and curled her finger at me.

I scooted in front of the fire next to her chair and propped my arm on the end table beside it.

"The power's in the message, not in the metal," she reminded me in a whisper.

"Oh yeah, that's right. Then . . . what *is* the message of a helmet and arm torn off an old patched suit of armor?"

"I think it has to do with the church."

That sounded kind of boring to me, but I didn't say so. The last thing I was *ever* going to do was hurt Reece's feelings again.

"Why here, though?" I asked. "What's so special about our town that *the very* armor of God—if that's what it is— would end up here?"

"The actual very armor of God is invisible, and anyone can have it. But why we have this, this . . ."

"Show-and-tell version?"

She thought a moment. "Yeah. That's a good way to put it. It's a real mystery, I'm beginning to see. Maybe a huge mystery, one that affects the whole world."

"Huh?"

"I just don't know. See, Jesus was born in Bethlehem and grew up in Nazareth."

I must have looked as blank as I did at my last pre-algebra pop quiz.

"Those were little nowhere towns, like Magdeline, which God chose for his purpose, so there must be a reason the armor of God ended up here." She leaned back and closed her eyes, but not in a sleepy way. *"Soterion. Koinonia,"* she said softly, and got this smile that's hard to describe. It's sort of like when you smell brownies baking, or the first time in spring when you can roll the windows down in the car and stick your head out and feel the sun and wind—that kind of smile.

I think she was praying.

Chapter 22

I put one last log on, drew the fire screen closed so no sparks could escape, and listened to Robbie snore until Reece woke up, or whatever you call it when you're done praying.

We have a bird clock at the lodge, which chirps a different birdcall every hour. The robin chirped, which meant it was 2:00 in the morning.

"A body detached from its head will die," she said plainly.

"Yeah . . ." I said back, grasping the obvious.

"Well, Jesus is the head of the church. The Bible says so. If the church separates from Jesus, it will die too."

Skid's eyes popped open and he practically yelped, "Whoa! Reece, I think you have it!"

I jumped. She sat up and leaned forward, curious and excited. "Elijah, didn't Mr. Dowland talk a lot about dinners and fancy programs at the church?"

"Yeah."

"But did he ever say anything about helping poor people or doing mission work or Bible study—anything like that?"

"No, nothing like that."

"Well, that doesn't necessarily mean the important stuff didn't happen, but if the minister was focused only on the partying, then the church wouldn't be a real church for long. It would turn into a club or a block party."

I wasn't really following her. "What about the arm piece? What does that mean?"

"Severed *koinonia,*" Skid said, turning his head toward us. "Somewhere along the way the church broke its connection with God."

"And with each other," Reece added. She must have seen the blank disappointment in my eyes. This didn't seem like much of a quest. "I know it sounds like no big deal, Elijah, but look what we've been through, some pretty heavy *koinonia* trouble ourselves. And it was just awful."

I remembered how my heart caught a bad case of the flu when I lost my friends. How would it be if a whole church full of people felt that way, all angry and sad, worse and worse for years? Pretty yuck. And a once-nice preacher turning into sour, crazy old Stan Dowland—the human face of Telanoo. Whoa . . .

"Skid, do you have the Quella?" Reece asked.

"Yup."

"Cross reference *koinonia.*"

"Sure." Half asleep, he pulled that little gold gizmo out of his jacket, slid his eyes open, and punched in some letters. It took a few minutes, but then he said, "How about this one? 'What fellowship can light have with darkness?' That's 2 Corinthians 6:14. Or . . ." He punched some more. "'If we claim to have fellowship with him yet walk in the darkness, we lie and do not live by the truth.' That's 1 John 1:6. I'll have to do more research, but it seems like when fellowship is broken people fall into darkness."

"Just look what happened to us," Reece said.

"Because of the armor?" I offered.

"No, because we were all wanting what we wanted. If we had found any kind of treasure, the same thing would have happened. Our problems weren't because of the armor, but because of how we treated each other in a crisis."

"Not so good," I admitted. "I thought we'd never be friends again. How did it get so messed up?"

"One bad apple spoils the whole bunch," said Skid. I was about to take offense when he added, "What if the bad apple in Old Pilgrim was the preacher himself? What if he started it all, but didn't turn things back around and make it right, like Elijah did with us?" He paused and turned to me. "Hey, I'm sorry if I made it hard on you."

"No prob."

Reece said, "We all did things without considering each other's feelings. I called in Skid because I knew he could be trusted. But no one else knew that."

"So the mystery of Old Pilgrim Church is solved, anyway. We know why it died. Basically it was beheaded," I said. "Hey, let me see that Quella thing? What's that mean? What is it?"

Eyes closed, Skid tossed it in my general direction. "The name's a take-off of a German word for source. The Quella's a combination Bible, concordance, lexicon, and encyclopedia. It's a prototype. I can't be hauling a ton of books around."

I fiddled with it.

"Cool, huh?" Reece said. "Facts from the most important ancient scrolls ever, high-tech access."

I punched keys. "But . . . why?"

"Answers," she said.

"Answers to what?"

"Oh, not much really," she teased. "Just life and death and eternity and supernatural powers—little piddly things like that."

The others drifted into sleep. I was the only one awake when the bird clock chirped 3:00 A.M. I turned my face to the dying embers, and bedded down. The door creaked. Wisps of cold air swept across the floor. The dark red coals flared. "Night, Bo," I whispered into the dark. He didn't answer.

I woke a couple of times later, when the cold wisps swept around me again.

Gray light came through the high windows of the lodge. One by one we roused.

We'd already decided that "we" would see where the other path in Telanoo led, but I didn't know how to break it to Reece that she couldn't make the trip, and she hadn't said anything either. I was sweating over how to handle the situation.

She sat up and stretched and said, "Off to Telanoo. What's the weather?"

She must have read shock on my face, though I was

straining to hide it. I guess that's why Robbie's the actor and I haul props.

"I'm going," she said.

"Sure, okay," I said in a fake cheery tone. "No prob."

"It will be a problem, Elijah, a big problem. You may have to carry me the whole way. But there's no way I'm not going."

"Yeah, that's fine. But, um, do you think you should call your mom or something, to make sure?"

"I already told her we might be going on a long hike, that you and Skid would take care of me. She said okay."

It wasn't that I was afraid of a little hard work. I just didn't want to be responsible for tripping across Telanoo with Reece riding piggyback and breaking every bone in her body. It was an established fact that I'm not the most graceful thing.

Dad came by and asked how we were.

Fine, I told him, and that Bo had looked in on us regularly all night.

"All night?" Dad said curiously.

"Yeah. He was in the office some, and the door kept opening and closing all night."

Dad grinned, "You must have dreamt it. When Bo saw you had settled down and drawn the fire screen, he left for the night."

He pulled a note out of his pocket, small and crumpled, and tossed it to me. It read: *3:00 A.M. The kids are down. All secured. I'm turning in. Bo.*

"Oh. I guess I was dreaming," I said casually, but I could have sworn the door had opened at least once more, right after the northern oriole on the bird clock chirped 6:00, and footsteps came over to where we slept, then back out with a rush of cold air. My face had been turned to the fire, my back to the door, and the sleeping bag pulled up high around my head, but still I would have sworn it.

"We're going on a hike. Is that okay?" I asked him.

Dad was halfway to the stairs. "Sure." Then he turned. "Just be on the lookout. Some dog got loose in Newpoint and bit a child. They haven't found it yet."

The five of us looked at each other. I hardly dared to ask, "What kind of dog?"

"A big black malamute, and not the best disposition, from what the neighbors said. It'll probably turn up in Newpoint, but just as a caution."

Robbie's eyes got big as saucers as he breathed the word, "Salem."

Chapter 23

AUNT Grace and Uncle Dorian were into antiquing, combing old properties for buried lockboxes and such. They weren't the least bit suspicious when Robbie asked his mom to drop off their metal detector. He told her we were hiking around, looking for ancient buried treasure, and she said, "Sure. If you find anything, I get ten percent."

Reece prayed for a clear, warm morning and we got one. I asked her why didn't she pray for that kind of day every day. She rolled those sky blue eyes at me and said, "It doesn't work that way, Elijah. God helps his children. He doesn't spoil them rotten. And can you imagine the earth with all sunny days and no rain? You know better than that."

She went on further to explain that prayers aren't all about getting what we want either. They should have in them somewhere "thy will be done." It seems prayers work best if that part's added in.

We took the golf cart as far as we could. Then we separated out our gear: detector, shovel, walkie-talkies, binoculars, canteen and sandwiches, and my bow and arrows—thrown in as an afterthought.

Reece could make it okay on the smoother parts. And we had plenty of rest stops along the way. None of us could shake the idea that the old man's riddle meant separate secrets were buried with each piece, and that each piece might be along the path through Telanoo. That's when Skid remembered a letter from Dr. Stallard. He pulled a folded envelope out of his jeans pocket and tore into it. "I wanted to open this when we were together. I totally forgot last night."

He read: *"Dear Marcus and other children, I have discovered a bit of interesting news you should know. A few of the links in the fragment of chain mail you gave me are pure gold."*

"Pure gold?" Robbie wheezed.

"Twenty-four carat," Skid read on. *"This is quite remarkable. From a defensive standpoint, this makes no sense, of course. Gold is a soft metal. Other alloys can be added to strengthen it. Sometimes pure gold is used with ornaments or overlays, say, on a ceremonial breastplate or sword hilt. But solid gold mesh in battle armor is unheard of. The weight—and therefore the value—of these links is insignificant. Also, from the small sampling we have, it's impossible to say whether the gold links are random or if they make a pattern, perhaps a symbol. Time will tell when the pieces come together. Destroy this note, and tell no one. Stay the course. Dr. Stallard."*

"We have to find it!" Robbie burst out, skipping ahead and acting like he had ants in his pants.

Conversation slacked off, as we needed all our breath to walk. We'd crossed what I guessed was a third of Telanoo when we found the forked path and headed in a northeast direction. *Get it.* The words I'd told myself that night at Great Oak came back to me strong and clear.

"We'll get it, no prob," I said confidently.

"But no more lying," Reece huffed and puffed.

"How can we keep it a secret, if we don't—?"

"No lying, no matter what. That's my final word."

I didn't see how that was possible, but kept my opinion to myself.

When the way got jagged and rough, Skid and I took turns carrying Reece piggyback. It was exhausting, but I didn't let on. A couple of times she whispered thanks and "You're really great to do this" and "This is the most fun I've had," even though she had to be in a lot of pain and really tired.

The whole time I kept my ear perked for bloodthirsty barking. I just couldn't get the idea of Salem on the loose out of my mind. So I stayed close to Mei, who carried my bow.

We came to a strangely slanted hill and slowly made our way up. From the top, the view stretched out on three sides. The girls oohed and aahed. In the distance smooth hills rolled between valleys thick with trees. A few tiny white farmhouses with red or black barns could be seen. In the center of the far panorama was a heavy woods stretching to the east as far as the eye could see.

"That's Council Cliffs State Park," I pointed.

Mei had never been there, so I described it: "It has water-carved gorges, a natural rock bridge, waterfalls, box canyons, and shallow caves where some believe Indian councils were held."

"We'll have to go there sometime," Reece said enthusiastically. Her cheeks were pink, though she was pale around the mouth. She'd never ever walked this far all at one time.

Everyone agreed that we'd hike the rim of a canyon next spring.

The trail went cold on that hill of nothing but rocks and hard-packed dirt. We wandered the hilltop for clues and came up with zip. Mei, who'd brought binoculars, scanned the wide meadow below us and the thickets beyond. Robbie suggested that he and I scout ahead while the others rested.

Half a dozen crows flew over and landed in the smooth, bleached branches of a lone sycamore at the highest point of the hill. Robbie called our attention to it and named it the Bone Tree. The crows screeched at us. According to some Indian beliefs, birds are the Great Spirit's way of acknowledging our presence. *If that's so,* I wondered, *are they saying hello, or warning us to go back?* I began to see why Indians read nature like a book.

The hill we stood on looked like no other in the whole area. It started down as a gentle curve, but it just kept curving— like a giant boulder—until it was almost straight down by the time it reached the meadow below. It was covered with thorns and decaying stumps, with cracks and crevices in the worst places for rock climbing. I worried how we'd all get down and if this even was the way. But this hilltop was where the path had led. I scouted around the hill a little, and was looking for a path down when Mei called out, "I see . . . a broken . . . house."

"A what?" I scrambled back up the hill and borrowed the binoculars.

If it hadn't been a sunny, leafless day, and if Mei hadn't been looking very hard, we'd never have found it. At the far end of the vast meadow, poking up just above a dark tangle of gnarly trees and bushes were the remains of a chimney and a wall. "It's a ruin!" I cried.

"Maybe that's it!" Robbie said. "Maybe the next grave is there! Let's go!"

I couldn't leave Reece behind, even though she knew how excited we were to get there quickly. She even kept saying, "You guys go on. You can describe it through the walkie-talkies. I can watch from here. Please, I want you to go ahead."

But it was so strong in my heart to bring her along that the extra half hour it would take wasn't important. That brave smile and sad slant in her eyes nailed it for me. If I was going, she was going. When I said so, her whole face lit up.

We all were scared going down the hill, an unnatural curve compared to the rest of the landscape, shaped like the back of a crusty old skull. Robbie came up with the name Devil's Cranium. Mei pretty much scooted down on her backside from rock to rock with our gear tucked under her arm or hanging from her neck. Even easygoing Skid clamped his jaw shut and didn't relax the whole way down. We formed a kind of box around Reece: Robbie went in front, with Skid and me on either side, inch by inch. Most of what we said on the way down was, "easy, easy, step here, yeah, good, okay, take it easy, good," and so on.

Reece was white as a sheet when we got to the bottom, but her smile was ear to ear. "Made it," she said, breathing hard. "Made it."

All of a sudden we were in a huddle, hugging and laughing, like we'd just won the World Series.

We didn't dare think how we were going to get back up that ripped and ragged place where nothing new grew. Nothing died there either, but just sort of hung on to life half-heartedly. Maybe the devil himself *was* buried up to his neck in Telanoo.

It was a ruin, all right, burned, decayed, overgrown. Only part of a charred creek stone chimney remained, with so much other stone scattered around the base we wondered if it had been a two-story house with an upstairs fireplace. Thickets of thorns swallowed the one upright corner of foot-thick logs. Strips of rusty metal and broken or melted glass crunched under our feet.

Quietly, we picked our way around the ruin, looking here and there for clues, wondering who had lived at the literal edge of nowhere, and why. We steered clear of the chimney, which was ready to topple any second. Beyond my surprise that someone had actually lived in Telanoo, I kept wondering if this location tied in to the armor.

Robbie showed Mei how to use the metal detector, and they found a few more metal strips buried under the dirt.

Chapter 23

We took a break. I built a fire on the old concrete stoop and made hot drinks for everyone from our canteen water. We had peanut butter sandwiches too. I went and sat by Reece on the corner logs, still finding it hard to believe that she was speaking to me again, much less was still my friend, still part of my clan. Forgiveness had to be the coolest thing ever, especially for people like me.

"Maybe the treasure's not here," she said tiredly. "Maybe it's back at Devil's Cranium, where the trail ended."

I hadn't thought of that. "Now that you mention it, Stan Dowland couldn't have made that cliff, do you think? He's seventy-eight."

She told the others what we were thinking.

Robbie said, "You mean to tell me . . . we climbed down that suicide hill, nearly broke our necks, for nothing?!"

I expected Reece to blow a fuse, to zing one of her sarcasms at me. Instead she started to smile, then broke into giggles. I started laughing too, and in a minute we were all cracking up . . . until I heard over our giggles what I'd listened for with dreaded anticipation all day. Echoing across the meadow came a fierce, raspy barking that chilled me right to the bone.

My head shot around. There on top of Devil's Cranium was an angry, jittery, black speck. "Salem," I breathed. "It's him!"

We watched the beast pace back and forth across the top of the hill, barking like mad, looking for a way down.

No, I said inside. *No. No!*

The black dot stopped pacing and raving across the top of Devil's Cranium and started in a fever to work its way down the pale gray slope. From such a great distance, Salem looked as harmless as a marble bouncing its way down through a pinball machine. But I'd seen those blazing eyes and dripping fangs bared and hungry for flesh. Everyone looked at me, and saw pure fear.

"Mei!" I yelled. "Where's my bow?!"

"I put it down!" she cried, and started running. "Oh, where is it? Where is it!?"

It seemed like hours, but a few seconds later she shoved the bow into my hand.

"The arrows! The arrows!" I yelled, my eyes still locked onto that dark spot. Salem had made it to the bottom of Devil's Cranium in precious little time. He disappeared in the tall, bleached grass of the meadow, but his fierce bark kept getting louder. We watched in horror as the tall grass quivered. It was like standing on the bow of a ship, watching a torpedo cut through water, aimed dead on for its target, unstoppable.

Salem had my scent.

I'd done a lot of target practice, but never at a swift moving thing. Never a thing coming at me at top speed. In a flash Mei thrust the quiver in my hand. I slung it over my shoulder.

"Get a weapon!" I yelled. "Everyone! Girls, get back!"

Robbie had the metal detector. He ran and stood on the porch slab and held it like a bat. Mei helped Reece up on a rock, then handed her a couple of small stones. She got stones too, and they stood together, their eyes wide with terror.

Skid came up to my side with the shovel, held like a spear. He shot me a look. "How's your aim?"

I drew the bow up and aimed at the approaching snake of quivering prairie grass. "Not bad."

I could see Salem's head now, hear him cutting through the dry grass, thrusting forward with power in every stride like a racehorse in the final stretch. I was his finish line. He was coming after me first, and then the others who carried my scent because they were my friends. My arms trembled under the tension of the bow.

Steady! Steady!

I had one chance, maybe two. The black malamute's loping head fully appeared in the thinning winter grass. I shot. I heard a yelp, but the face kept coming. I pulled another arrow, drew back, aimed, shot.

Missed.

"One more!" yelled Skid.

Salem, the guardian of the curse of Old Pilgrim Church, was in full view now, his wild glowing eyes fixed, fangs bared. I'd broken into his house and he was coming to settle the score.

For the first time in my life, time stretched itself out. Sound stopped. I couldn't hear him ripping through the grass any longer, his vicious barks faded. I saw no hill or meadow or sky, nothing but a gaping, fanged mouth coming at me, dead in my sight.

Aim . . . aim . . .

We locked eyes. He came off the ground in slow motion.

Shoot!

I released. The arrow cut through the air and penetrated his mouth. He yelped, a black bulk writhing in mid-air, still hurling himself at me. I jumped back, but his body caught me on the shins. I stumbled backward. Skid attacked the thrashing, howling creature, jabbing the blade of the shovel into its neck and side. I recovered my balance, drew another arrow and released it into the creature's spine. He went berserk, clawing and gnawing at the arrow shaft sticking out of his mouth.

"Turn him over!" I yelled to Skid, drawing another arrow. "I need a shot at his belly!"

"Can't!" he yelled back. But gathering courage he took aim, rushed forward, and thrust the shovel into the beast's side, sending him sprawling. Swiftly I moved in, crouched, positioned the point of my arrow inches from his heart, drew back the bow, and released. A howl, then a whimper escaped through the stream of blood spewing from his mouth.

It was gruesome, what my arrows and Skid's shovel did to that beast of a dog.

Time resumed. I looked around to the others. They had been screaming and crying, I guessed, but I hadn't heard it.

Now the sounds came rushing back. My head spun dizzily. I breathed. "It's okay," I said. "We got him."

Mei had the hiccups from crying. Robbie stayed frozen in place with the metal detector held over his shoulder like a bat, until I went over and pried his fingers loose. Reece was a terrible shade of white.

"You okay?" I asked her.

She smiled at me, trembling. "I'm good."

When Salem was altogether dead and finished twitching, we approached him in a clump, all moving together like we had in the church basement—only this time with *five* heads and *ten* feet—until we stood over his bludgeoned remains.

No one said anything for a long time. We all seemed to realize that this wasn't just about a mean dog getting loose in the neighborhood.

"Dowland let him loose on us," Skid said quietly.

As one, our heads went up, our eyes on the far crest of Devil's Cranium. We scanned the edge of the cliff for the old man. But he wasn't there.

"We need to get out of here," I said. "Gather your things."

Reece stood staring at the hill for a long time, while the rest of us hurried to leave. She came up to me, her eyes full of tears. "Elijah, it just occurred to me, just this second: what if you hadn't brought me down with you, what if I'd stayed . . ." she turned to the hill, "up there?"

The others overheard. It struck us all, the grief of what might have happened . . . the four of us watching helplessly from the meadow while far away, up on that hill, all alone and defenseless, Reece . . . I can't even say what would have happened, it's so horrible.

But I couldn't take credit for saving her. "I felt it strong that you should come, Reece. Something told me not to leave you there."

I think I grew up a whole year in that one minute.

Chapter 24

WE left Salem's body draining blood onto the hard, cold ground of the ruin.

On the way back across the long meadow, I asked Reece what *maranatha* meant.

"It means 'our Lord comes.' It's a word of victory and encouragement."

I rolled it around on my tongue. "Sounds Indian."

"Aramaic," Skid murmured.

"The language Jesus spoke two thousand years ago," Reece explained.

"No one speaks Aramaic anymore?" I assumed.

"Not around here," said Skid with a sly smile.

"Do you?" I asked him.

"Talitha koum."

"Show-off," I said tiredly.

He laughed. "I only know that one phrase because it's in the Bible. It means 'little girl, get up.' Jesus said it to a dead girl when he brought her back to life."

I laughed. "A dead girl made alive?"

"Yeah," said Skid.

"You say it like it's no big deal."

He shot me a direct look. "It isn't, not to him."

The climb back up Devil's Cranium was a piece of cake compared to what we'd just been through. Robbie reminded us of the old movie. With crows crying above our heads on that curved gray stone cliff, a screaming skull wasn't much off the mark.

When we'd made it up to the Bone Tree and had caught our breaths, I asked if anyone had heard footsteps or felt a draft in the lodge after 3:00 the night before. No, they said, but they knew where this was heading.

Skid looked out over the meadow. "If it wasn't Bo, and it wasn't your dad . . ."

"Dowland was in the room?!" Reece cried.

"While we were sleeping!?" Mei added.

Robbie looked at me wildly. "Hold on! Did you ever find my cap, the one I lost at the fence?"

"No, and . . . I have to confess here and now. That night we saw Dowland in the graveyard I never said anything, Robbie, but Dowland probably did see us. He may have found your cap, taken it—"

"—to give Salem my scent!"

We were creeped out at the possibility that Dowland had been plotting against us from the very first. But at the same time, we were more determined than ever to follow our instincts and see where they led us.

The trail did seem to end at the top of the hill. All around was rock and scrub grass. Even the five of us tromping around the entire cusp of the hill hadn't left a print. So now what?

Remembering the medicine ways of the Indians, I wondered out loud if the crows were a sign, and I got ready to hear a sermon about what a silly idea it was. But Reece surprised me.

"'Ask the animals, and they will teach you, or the birds of the air, and they will tell you; or speak to the earth, and it will teach you.' That's in the book of Job. See, everything belongs to God, Elijah. He created everything; breathed life into it. He can use what he likes, when he likes, to teach us about himself."

I hopped to attention like a soldier. "Okay, then, we'll take a clue from the crows and start at the Bone Tree, where they landed and where the trail ended. Let's get the metal detector going. We'll start at the trunk and move out in a systematic way."

While Mei and Robbie worked, Skid and I kept our senses tuned for any sign of life approaching the hill. Skid found a stick to use as a club. I was armed and ready with my bow.

Reece rested and told me how God used a dove and a raven after the flood, and how Jesus used sparrows in a sermon on how God cares for people. A faraway look came over her face. "I've never told anyone but Mom, but the week before my dad left, a pair of doves built a nest right outside my window. They sat on the branch and just stared at the house. A month later they kicked the nest apart and flew away." Her eyes got misty and she turned to me and smiled. "My mom said maybe God was teaching us lessons: that homes could be easily made and easily broken, and that God knew our home was being broken. He was there watching."

I wanted to ask why didn't he do something if he was really God, but I could tell it was hard for her to say even that much.

"So that stuff about learning from the animals—that's in the Bible?" I asked.

"You might be surprised what's in there," she said with a flirty kind of smile, wiping her eyes. She took a deep breath.

While Reece talked about the Bible, I kept an eye on Robbie and Mei using the metal detector, to make sure they didn't miss a spot. They circled the tree, working their way out in bigger and bigger circles. The ground was lumpy with rocks scattered and in piles here and there, as if it could have been recently disturbed. On a bare hill exposed to the weather, a spot of freshly dug earth would have settled soon enough. I went picking around the tree ahead of Robbie, when I noticed a cluster of moldy rocks. The odd thing was that some had mold on top, while some were bare on top with mold growing on the underside.

"Somebody turned these stones over. Fairly recently. Hey, guys, I think I found something." The others gathered around. The sunny morning was long gone by that time. A cold front had moved in. I shivered.

Mei pointed the metal detector and began scanning. "Here!" she said excitedly.

Without a word, Robbie and I kicked aside stray stones

and made a bare spot. I grabbed the shovel and jammed the blade into the ground. Setting my shoe on the head of the blade, I actually wanted to say some kind of prayer. Reece had said "thy will be done" works good, so I said it under my breath and put my weight into the shovel.

We took turns being lookouts and diggers. The dirt was rocky and coarse; it was painstaking work. Each time that shovel hit dry grit and stone, I hoped for the resistance of burlap. But nothing. Down two feet and counting, shovel after shovel . . . nothing . . . more nothing . . . then . . .

"Hit something!" I said, tossing the shovel aside and dropping to my knees. Robbie and Skid joined me and we dug with our hands. When Robbie's hand swept across burlap, we let out a whoop. It was as good as gold to us.

"Let Mei get it," Reece said quietly.

We stopped. She was telling us nicely to back off and let Mei get a piece of the action. And she was right. Mei was shy and always took a back seat to whatever the rest of the group wanted to do.

"Sure," Skid said. "Mei, you get it out."

"No, go ahead," Mei said.

"No, you can," Reece said. "I want you to be part of it too."

Slowly she nodded and smiled.

Ever so carefully she lifted it out.

At first we thought the bag was empty. There was no bulk or weight to it.

"It's empty," Robbie whined, then his eyes lit up and he said, "No, wait! It's just like Dowland did before. Remember, he buried the pieces deep and threw the bag on top. We're going to have to dig more."

Mei lifted the sack out by two fingers of each hand. "Something is in here. Reece?"

With a gasp of pain, Reece got down on her knees and reached out for the sack. Mei put it in her hands. Carefully she ran her hand under the burlap to feel the shape of its contents. She didn't tear into the sack, like I expected. She looked up knowingly and smiled. "Of course."

"What is it?" I asked.

"It's the belt of truth. I know it, even before looking."

My shoulders slumped. I'd hoped it was the helmet and arm piece.

"Oh, don't be discouraged, Elijah," she said. "It's the first one."

"What do you mean?"

"The first one listed in the Bible. We were supposed to start with this piece, after all," she beamed. "See, it makes perfect sense too. If we had found the belt first, we might not have thought anything of it. Just an old belt in a sack. But finding the helmet first, having it for a while, was like a hint. The helmet was to spur us on to search for the rest."

"When do we find the helmet again?" I asked impatiently. "Which number is it?"

She thought back. "It's the fifth piece, right before the

sword." She looked around at all of us. "Don't you see? We will find it all. We have to!"

Every emotion in the world swept through me. I'd hoped we had rediscovered the helmet and arm piece, for sure. I wanted to redeem the pieces I'd lost. But when she said this was the first piece mentioned in the Bible, it did seem to me as if our feet were set on a definite course, an honest-to-goodness quest.

I knelt beside her. "The belt of truth . . . so, what's that mean?"

Her answer—when she finally said it—sent a thrill and a chill right through me.

She pierced into me with those sky-blue eyes, with the wind blowing her hair back from her face, her expression holding all sorts of kindness, but ruthlessness and courage too.

Reece said, "It means, Elijah Creek, that whatever plans you had for your life . . . well, that's all about to change."

THE ANCIENT OMEN

THERE we were under the Bone Tree with a muddy sack we'd just dug out of Devil's Cranium. The sunny day Reece had prayed for suddenly turned blustery and cold. Wind cut like razors across that hill and right through our jackets. We kept low to the ground on our hands and knees around the spot where the metal detector had beeped.

Mei put on plastic gloves—like we'd decided to do when handling the artifacts—as if we were investigating a crime. We held our breaths as Mei slowly reached into the sack. Something small and round fell out. It was a broken compass.

Weeks before, we'd found the helmet and right arm of the armor of God, which had long ago been buried in the basement of Old Pilgrim Church, and which old Stan Dowland had dug up and re-buried near the cemetery. The rest of it was still at large. We had ourselves a mystery involving two ancient relics, maybe worth a fortune. But thanks to my stupidity we had lost them, with little hope of ever finding them again. Only a thousand-year-old scrap of chain mail remained, and it was now in the hands of a scientist in Chicago by the name of Stallard.

It was clear that this was a quest, and that all of us—but especially me, Elijah Creek—had been chosen for it. Reece came to that conclusion after I told her about my night alone in The Cedars when a Bible verse came ringing inside my head: *Put on the full armor of God.* That kind of thing had never happened to me before.

So I became head of this operation.

The rest of the group on the quest were Reece and her Japanese friend Mei, my cousin Robbie, and Skid. I don't mind saying I wasn't thrilled about letting Skid into our group. But he was useful. He found Stanford Dowland, the key to our quest; and Skid made connections with Dr. Stallard, who advised us to keep quiet about the armor until further notice. Skid was convinced the scientist could be trusted.

Mei laid the compass in her palm and we all leaned in. It was rusty and the glass was shattered and mostly gone.

"Is that it?" Skid asked. "That's no relic."

"I thought you said you felt a belt in there," Robbie snipped.

Reece was still holding the sack. "It's in here. Has to be. Get it out, Mei."

Mei laid the compass down and looked in the sack again.

"It is a belt!" she said.

The wind swept over us, building as it blew across the dead meadows of Telanoo. We braced ourselves against it and studied the belt. It didn't look ancient, but it wasn't modern either. It was a leather strip about the width of your hand. The buckle was strange: a metal plate with rough lumps and lines, like it had been hammered into shape. On either side of the buckle was faded tapestry material.

"Those designs, do they look Indian to you?" I asked.

"Maybe African," said Mei, "or from the Middle East."

Odd-shaped pieces of metal were strung around the back of the belt on leather laces.

"Yes!" Reece looked at it lovingly. Her breathing was uneven. I thought she might faint.

"You okay?" I asked.

"We will find all of it," she said with conviction. "It may take a while, but we will find the whole armor of God."

For a long time she knelt over the belt, easing the dust and dirt off. "*Aletheia,*" she whispered excitedly.

Skid repeated it, and they looked at each other across the dig, their eyes all glittery. *Skid and Reece and their blasted secret bond!*

"What?" I asked, scooting over beside her. "You see something?"

"Truth." Reece smiled at me. "The belt should say *aletheia,* which is 'truth' in Greek."

"How do you know that?" I asked.

"The other two pieces had Greek engravings, so I looked up all the words from Ephesians chapter six that describe the armor."

Reece's leg was killing her and she needed to stand. She handed the belt back to Mei, and I helped her up. We all examined the belt, hoping to see the same kind of letters we'd seen on the other pieces: the helmet of *soterion,* or "salvation," and the right arm piece engraved with the word *koinonia,* "fellowship."

Mei picked away the mud caked on the buckle. "Is this a word . . . or a symbol?"

"It has to be the belt of truth!" Reece cried.

Skid tried to be encouraging. "Does it have to have the word on it?"

Reece said, "It should. Truth doesn't hide."

Huge gusts of wind slammed into the hill, stronger with each slam. The last one almost knocked us over. Mother Nature had taken up bowling and we were the pins.

"We gotta get out of here!" I yelled over the wind. "C'mon!" Getting Reece over the rocks and across the rutted terrain of Telanoo was going to take a while.

Time and time again I'd asked about who owned this land northeast of the camp. Once Dad said, "Oh, it's probably part of the Morgan farm." Another time he said, "Maybe Old Pilgrim Church owns it." Then another time, "Could be part of Council Cliffs State Park. I'm not sure, Elijah." I'd asked others and gotten the same runaround. Bo, the camp activities and security director said, "There's nothing back there." Mrs. Horstley who does office work at camp said, "Well, I don't really know, hon, but it couldn't be near as pretty and nice as the campgrounds. If you see 'No Trespassing' signs back there, you should stay out." Never a real answer. There were no signs, nothing to keep me out or fight against my crazy curiosity to prowl about whenever I had the chance.

The five of us made the long hike back to the golf cart in good time. Reece walked much better on the way out than she had on the way in. Maybe it was the excitement of finding another piece of the armor. We loaded ourselves and our gear into the golf cart. As we zipped along the paved path through Owl Woods, we talked about where to take our treasure for a closer look. Once in plain sight of the camp buildings, it hit me: the camp was busy on all fronts today. I yelled above the roar of the wind and the cart's motor, "We've got to find another place! Camp's busting at the seams. High school retreat in the front cabins, historical meeting at the lodge, Pioneer Days for middle schoolers at the shelter house. And . . . oh no . . ."

A dead serious look must have washed over my face.

"Elijah! What's wrong?" Reece asked.

"The Mad River Boys are coming later on. I just remembered."

"Mad River Boys?" Reece asked.

"From the boys' ranch upstate. A reform school. Big trouble! Dad has to put them in the back cabins!"

We burst out of the shelter of the woods into the wintry blast again. Skid tucked the sack into his black suede jacket, buttoning it up to his neck.

Reece and Mei were shivering but not complaining. The smell of snow was in the air. I went full throttle around the lake trail toward home. "I'll let you out at my house. You guys scope out the situation there while I drop off the cart."

Ancient Truth

(*page 82*) "Therefore put on the full armor of God, so that when the day of evil comes, you may be able to stand your ground, and after you have done everything, to stand. Stand firm then, with the belt of truth buckled around your waist, with the breastplate of righteousness in place, and with your feet fitted with the readiness that comes from the gospel of peace. In addition to all this, take up the shield of faith, with which you can extinguish all the flaming arrows of the evil one. Take the helmet of salvation and the sword of the Spirit, which is the word of God."

Ephesians 6:13-17

(*page 106*) "Simply let your 'Yes' be 'Yes,' and your 'No,' 'No'; anything beyond this comes from the evil one."

Matthew 5:37

(*page 160*) "What do righteousness and wickedness have in common? Or what fellowship can light have with darkness?"

2 Corinthians 6:14

(*page 160*) "If we claim to have fellowship with him yet walk in the darkness, we lie and do not live by the truth."

1 John 1:6

(*page 179*) "Ask the animals, and they will teach you,
or the birds of the air, and they will tell you;
or speak to the earth, and it will teach you,
or let the fish of the sea inform you."

Job 12:7, 8

Greek Code

※※

Japanese Words

Daijoubu—(die-jo-boo) It's all right

Mei Aizawa—(May I-zawa)

Sugoi—(soo-goy) Wow

Taihen—(tie-hen) Terrible; very, etc. (as in terrible or terribly pretty)

Greek Words

Koinonia—fellowship

Maranatha—our Lord comes

Soterion—salvation

Aramaic

Talitha koum—little girl, get up

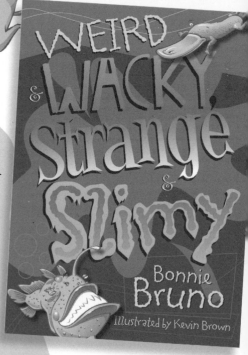